"Why are you so anxious to run from me? You do not take my proposition seriously?"

"You want me to marry you?" Just saying the words sent a shiver down Olivia's spine, her thoughts flying in a hopeless direction. "Why? Do you love me?"

"I have a great fondness for you."

"Why?"

"Your violet eyes. They intrigue me. And you will bear many brave, strong-willed children."

She blinked. "I thought you didn't want any. In fact, last night you said—"

"I am not a patient man, Olivia."

It wasn't her imagination that he moved closer, or that his eyes had darkened. "Is that supposed to win me over?"

"Perhaps this will." He cupped her nape, drawing her closer, and covered her mouth with his.

Dear Reader,

Heartwarming, emotional, compelling…these are all words that describe Harlequin American Romance. Check out this month's stellar selection of love stories, which are sure to delight you.

First, Debbi Rawlins delivers the exciting conclusion of Harlequin American Romance's continuity series, TEXAS SHEIKHS. In *His Royal Prize*, sparks fly immediately between dashing sheikh Sharif and Desert Rose ranch hand Olivia Smith. However, Sharif never expected their romantic tryst to be plastered all over the tabloids—or that the only way to salvage their reputations would be to make Olivia his royal bride.

Bestselling author Muriel Jensen pens another spectacular story in her WHO'S THE DADDY? miniseries with *Daddy To Be Determined*, in which a single gal's ticking biological clock leads her to convince a single dad that he's the perfect man to father her baby. In *Have Husband, Need Honeymoon*, the third book in Rita Herron's THE HARTWELL HOPE CHESTS miniseries, Alison Hartwell thought her youthful marriage to an air force pilot had been annulled, but surprise! Now a forced reunion with her "husband" has her wondering if a second honeymoon couldn't give them a second chance at forever. And Harlequin American Romance's promotion THE WAY WE MET…AND MARRIED continues with *The Best Blind Date in Texas*. Don't miss this wonderful romance from Victoria Chancellor.

It's a great lineup, and we hope you enjoy them all!

Wishing you happy reading,

Melissa Jeglinski
Associate Senior Editor
Harlequin American Romance

TEXAS SHEIKHS:
HIS ROYAL PRIZE
Debbi Rawlins

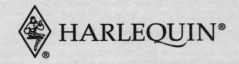

HARLEQUIN®

TORONTO • NEW YORK • LONDON
AMSTERDAM • PARIS • SYDNEY • HAMBURG
STOCKHOLM • ATHENS • TOKYO • MILAN • MADRID
PRAGUE • WARSAW • BUDAPEST • AUCKLAND

Special thanks and acknowledgment are given to Debbi Rawlins for her contribution to the Texas Sheikhs series.

In memory of Sister John Olivia. I miss you.

ISBN 0-373-16881-0

HIS ROYAL PRIZE

Copyright © 2001 by Harlequin Books S.A.

Visit us at www.eHarlequin.com

Printed in U.S.A.

ABOUT THE AUTHOR

Debbi Rawlins currently lives with her husband and dog in Las Vegas, Nevada. A native of Hawaii, she married on Maui and has since lived in Cincinnati, Chicago, Tulsa, Houston, Detroit and Durham, North Carolina, during the past twenty years. Now that she's had enough of the gypsy life, it'll take a crane, a bulldozer and a forklift to get her out of her new home. Good thing she doesn't like to gamble. Except maybe on romance.

Books by Debbi Rawlins

HARLEQUIN AMERICAN ROMANCE
580—MARRIAGE INCORPORATED
618—THE COWBOY AND THE CENTERFOLD
622—THE OUTLAW AND THE CITY SLICKER
675—LOVE, MARRIAGE AND OTHER CALAMITIES
691—MARRY ME, BABY
730—THE BRIDE TO BE...OR NOT TO BE
741—IF WISHES WERE...HUSBANDS
780—STUD FOR HIRE?
790—OVERNIGHT FATHER
808—HIS, HERS AND THEIRS
860—LOVING A LONESOME COWBOY
881—HIS ROYAL PRIZE

HARLEQUIN INTRIGUE
587—HER MYSTERIOUS STRANGER

TEXAS SHEIKHS

Habib Bin Mohammed El Jeved (King of Sorajhee)

Azzam m. Layla
{ Badia   Fayza   Jamila }

Ibrahim m. Rose Coleman

① Alim
(aka Alex Coleman)

③ Makin
(aka Mac Coleman)

② Kadar
(aka Cade Coleman) —— (aka Cade Coleman)

④ Sharif Asad Al Farid*

Randy and Virginia Coleman
{ Jessica }
(Don't miss her story coming in 2002)

Legend:
—— Twins
* Stolen at birth

① HIS INNOCENT TEMPTRESS 4/01
② HIS ARRANGED MARRIAGE 5/01
③ HIS SHOTGUN PROPOSAL 6/01
④ HIS ROYAL PRIZE 7/01

Chapter One

America was a strange and bewildering place. Sharif Asad Al Farid squinted out the parlor window at the vast expanse of the Desert Rose ranch. In the distance, he could see two of his three brothers working with the horses. Brothers he had just met, had not known existed until a week ago.

No, America was not so strange. Sharif had traveled to New York often while he studied at the university in London, and he had always enjoyed his visits. It was Texas that seemed odd to him, and the way his brothers embraced manual labor, even though they shared the same royal blood that flowed through his veins.

Did they not understand what it meant to be heir to the throne of Sorajhee? To be sons of a king?

Sharif massaged the tension knotting the back of his neck. More confusing than a desert mirage were the thoughts spinning incessantly like a whirlpool inside his head. He was not sure who he was anymore, or from where he truly came. For twenty-nine years he had been the firstborn, the only son of King Zakariyya and Queen Nadirah of Balahar. There had been no question he would ascend the throne. But now...

His glance slid to Rose, the American woman who

had borne him. She looked his way, her anxious blue eyes meeting his, and she stopped pouring tea. Her lips curved slightly. Only politeness made him return the tentative smile before he turned to stare out the window again.

He was a fool not to have guessed he had been adopted. Or that he was of half-Western ancestry. All the signs were in evidence—the lighter eyes, the fairer skin. Although his eyes were a dark midnight-blue and not as pale as those of this woman who claimed to be his mother, he in no way resembled King Zak's or Queen Nadirah's dark, regal looks.

There was a trace of English blood in Nadirah's lineage they had said—an explanation he had easily accepted. They were his parents. Why would he not have trusted them to speak the truth?

Bitterness taunted him, but he would not succumb. He understood the reason they had withheld the truth. The politics and public temperament of the time had prevented them from publicizing the verity of his birth—that he had secretly taken the place of their still-born child. They had protected him, protected his rightful place on the throne.

Rightful place. His insides clenched painfully, yet still the numbness threatened to engulf him. He almost welcomed the oblivion. What was his destiny? All his life he had been so sure of himself, his future as king. No more.

His belly cramped again. Uncertainty was such a difficult pill to swallow.

"Your mother is speaking to you," he heard King Zak say, and Sharif turned slowly toward his father. His adoptive father. The only one he had ever known.

Sharif wanted to tell him not to refer to this woman

as his mother. Queen Nadirah was dead and buried for several years now. But she had been the one to sit at the edge of his bed when fever raged through his young body, or when his knees had been skinned raw from scaling the palace walls. He missed her every day.

"I beg your forgiveness," Sharif said with stilted politeness. "My mind was wandering."

Rose smiled. "That's okay. I only asked what you'd like in your tea."

He eyed the tray of cups she had filled with the amber liquid. In her hand was a small porcelain bowl of sugar. It trembled slightly. "Do you not have servants to do this?"

She blinked, a startled look crossing her face. "There's a cook and housekeeper, and ranch hands to help with the horses, of course," she said slowly, "but not the kind of servants you're talking about." A smile tugged at her mouth. It gave beauty to her weary features. "It's been a long time since I've had anyone wait on me."

Stung by the reminder of her appalling imprisonment for the past twenty-nine years, Sharif's gaze quickly slid away. Right into his father's disapproving face.

King Zak's dark eyes narrowed, and he gestured toward the space beside him on the burgundy couch across from Rose. "Why do you not sit here with us? What is outside that so captures your attention?"

Sharif remained stubbornly silent for a few moments and then said, "I would like Scotch instead of the tea, if you have it."

"Of course." Rose immediately stood, ignoring Sharif's father's sound of disgust. "King Zakariyya? How about you?"

"Thank you." King Zak had risen, and he bowed

slightly. "But I do not make it a practice to drink before six o'clock."

Sharif got the message of his father's disapproval. He noted something else, as well. That King Zak could not seem to take his eyes off the American woman as she left the room.

Distaste surged through Sharif. "I think I will go for a ride. I assume there is someone around who can saddle a horse for me."

"Sharif, we have been here only one day. Your mother is trying very hard to make you welcome. Be kind to her."

He turned to stare out the window again. "My mother is in the ground."

King Zak sighed. "We should have told you the truth sooner. Until not long ago I did not know your mother was still alive. Do not punish her for my error in judgment."

Sharif stared off in the direction where Rose had disappeared in search of his Scotch. "She is very beautiful." He meaningfully met his father's eyes. "Is she not?"

After a long pause, King Zak said, "She has suffered greatly, locked away in the sanitarium for so many years because of a madwoman's thirst for power. She did not abandon you and your brothers. It is because of her sacrifices that you are all still alive. Royal blood may not flow through her veins, but she has the wisdom and strength of a true queen. You should be very proud to be her son."

There was truth in his father's words, Sharif knew. Rose had been a queen once, when she had married Ibrahim, Sharif's birth father, and ruler of Sorajhee. She had possessed power and fortune herself, along with her brother, Randy, the heirs of a wealthy and important American businessman.

When Ibrahim was assassinated, it was Randy in America to whom she had sent Sharif's three brothers for safekeeping while she sought the truth behind her husband's death. Before she could attain her goal, she was committed to a sanitarium in Europe.

Sharif still did not know all the details. Only that he was born five months later, then taken from Rose and given to his parents. Everyone had thought Rose was dead. Even her brother. Until recently. She had not lived an easy life. And for that misfortune, he pitied her. He even admired her strength and courage. But he was not yet ready to embrace her as family.

"I found the Scotch," she said, smiling as she reentered the room, a bottle of fine aged Scotch in one hand, a crystal tumbler in the other. "I hope this suits you."

Everything at the ranch was of the finest quality: the furnishings, the art adorning the walls, even the china and crystal. The Spanish-style house itself was solid and spacious and possessed over a dozen bedrooms that overlooked a glorious lake. And the Arabian horses housed in the stables were of superb breeding. His brothers certainly had not grown up wanting. Still, none of this compared to the opulent palace where Sharif had spent his twenty-nine years.

He wasn't sure how that made him feel, or why it mattered. All three of his brothers seemed content. Genuinely happy. Sharif was the one who was suffocating from confusion.

After accepting the glass of Scotch Rose poured, he downed the liquor in one gulp. "I will go for that ride now,'' he said, and stoically met her startled eyes. ''What time shall I return for dinner?''

''Sharif.'' His father's sharp tone shook the air like sudden thunder on a clear night.

Rose laid a hand on King Zak's arm, and his expression immediately softened. ''We eat around seven. But it'll start getting dark before then, so be careful.''

For a moment, his father's gaze lingered on the American woman, and Sharif's insides twisted at the longing he saw in those dark eyes. Anger and resentment sliced through him like a thief's sharpened dagger.

''I shall not be dining with you tonight.'' Sharif walked toward the French doors without another glance at them. ''Be certain my bedchamber has been made ready for my return.''

Even at his father's grunt of disapproval, he did not turn around. He continued out the door, and waved for his personal attendant to lag behind when the man rushed to accompany him. Sharif did not want anyone to see the pain his eyes surely could not hide.

''HE'S VERY ARROGANT.'' Rose watched her youngest son stride proudly away, his head held high, his posture perfectly erect. When she realized what she'd said, heat flared in her cheeks and her gaze flew to King Zak's face. ''I'm sorry. I didn't mean to sound critical. I was merely making an observation, really. You've done a fine job with him. And you have my everlasting thanks. He is very well mannered and bright and handsome...''

King Zak smiled. ''It is you who is responsible for his comeliness. He looks very much like you.''

Rose blushed again. ''Thank you, but I think he looks more like Ibrahim.'' Her gaze strayed out the window and she watched the way one shoulder dipped ever so slightly as Sharif walked. Remarkably like Ibrahim.

The memory of her husband was a knife in her heart, as though it had been only yesterday that his young life had been violently ripped away from hers.

"You are quite right," King Zak said, drawing her attention again. He had a fierce, swarthy look, but kind eyes. "Sharif is sometimes arrogant. We indulged him too much. Especially Nadirah. She awaited a child for a very long time."

He fell silent, staring out the window toward Sharif's disappearing form, and Rose knew he was thinking about his wife, missing her, as Rose still missed Ibrahim.

"This behavior…" he said finally, waving a ringed hand, a large ruby catching the sunlight and sparking brilliant red flames. "It is not so much arrogance as it is fear."

"Fear? Of me?"

"Of change."

"Oh, King Zakariyya, I don't expect anything to change. I want to be in his life, of course, but—"

"Please." He took one of her nervous hands and sandwiched it between his. "It is not necessary to be so formal. And Zak is so much easier on the tongue, is it not?"

She nodded, and willed her cheeks not to color as she extracted her hand as gracefully as she could. "I hope he understands that I don't expect him to welcome me overnight. I simply wish for the chance to get to know him, just as I've been getting to know the other boys."

"He is a good man. A true king. But right now his

identity is shaken. He needs some time. He is still growing up, I am afraid, but he would never let our people down. And he will not let you down. I am certain of this.''

As they both turned toward the window again, Rose prayed Zak was right. Sharif had already disappeared from sight. She felt his absence clear down to her soul.

''DAMN IT, LIVY, YOU CHEATED.''

Olivia Smith stopped laughing and glared at her friend and fellow ranch hand. ''Mickey Farrel, you worm, I've never cheated once in my life, and you know it. Take it back.''

''I won't.'' He stooped to pick his hat off the barn floor and shook the hay off the battered gray rim before setting the Stetson back on his head.

She had a good mind to knock his hat off again. He was twenty-two, just a year younger than she, but he acted as if he were twelve. ''Don't try and weasel out of mucking out the stalls. You lost fair and square.''

''How come I always lose? Tell me that. You *have* to be cheating.''

''That's the dumbest thing I ever heard.'' She walked over to get the shovel and thrust it at him. ''The object is to knock the other person's hat off without bodily contact. Which is exactly what I do. How could I possibly cheat?''

''All I know is I'm five foot ten and you're only five two. So how in the blazes do you always whack my hat off first?''

''It's called having a brain. Maybe you ought to use yours sometimes.''

Mickey muttered a foul word under his breath and grudgingly grabbed the shovel. ''Why can't you act like other girls, and not be such a tomboy and a bully?''

''I'm not a bully. You're just a sore loser,'' she said with a smug toss of her head so he wouldn't know how much the remark stung. The truth was, she'd grown up with mostly boys at the orphanage where she'd been abandoned as a baby and she wasn't sure she knew how to act like a girl.

Sometimes she wished she did know the right things to say, and had the proper clothes to wear, instead of her usual jeans and baggy shirts. Especially since Rose Coleman–El Jeved came to the ranch. She was so beautiful and poised that it was easy to imagine her as a queen just like in the fairy tales Livy read to the kids when she visited the orphanage. Except Rose had been a real life queen with a palace and servants and fine clothes and…

Livy straightened and grabbed her gloves. Wouldn't Mickey and the rest of the guys laugh themselves silly if they knew about her foolish daydreams. ''See you later,'' she said. ''I'll be working with Khalid.''

Mickey stared, slack jawed. ''You're not leaving me to muck out all thirty stalls by myself.''

''Be grateful you don't have all sixty to clean.'' She strode off before she gave in and helped him as she usually did. She had something else in mind. Although she really did plan on working with Khalid, the ranch's newest colt, she needed to stop and talk to her own horse first.

She swore that Prince was the only creature on God's green earth that understood her. Of course they shared a similar past. He'd been a runt, unwanted and shunned by breeders. Her parents had dumped her on the steps of St. Mary's before she could even talk.

Which was sort of a blessing. She obviously hadn't said anything bad that ticked them off or made them not want her. Reminding herself of that helped when she felt down and alone sometimes.

As soon as she saw Prince stick his head out of his stall, she broke into a grin. Now Prince Charming here had shown all the naysayers a thing or two. He'd turned into a fine stallion. Even some of the trainers and breeders who'd snubbed him earlier had changed their tune and offered her a heap of cash for him. It made her burst with pride. Not that she'd ever sell him in a million years. Even though he'd cost her every dime she'd saved.

"How ya doing, boy?" She reached into her pocket for his daily cube of sugar while she stroked his neck with her other hand. "You look mighty handsome today, young man." She laughed when he nuzzled her neck. "Thanks, but you still get only one cube."

She led him out of the stall and into the outdoor riding ring. The sun was low enough that it wasn't too hot, and she really wished she had the time to take him out for a good run. In another week the annual Hill Country Breakneck Race was going to make her and Prince a small fortune. Assuming they won. Although she had little doubt they would. Prince was that fast.

He was smart, too, and eventually she'd probably show him, just as Mac Coleman, the head trainer at the ranch, suggested.

"Come on, boy. Let's see what you remember." She led him around the ring at a slow pace. Sunlight gleamed off his shiny black coat. He looked like velvet in motion and her heart swelled with pride.

After a few more turns, she shaded her eyes and looked at the pink-streaked horizon. The sun was still visible, but she guessed it was about four-thirty or five. She had to go work with Khalid. Prince sensed he was about to be penned again and pulled back a little.

"I'm sorry, boy, I wish I could stay longer." She stroked the side of his neck, whispering to him in the low murmuring tone he liked. "If I don't work, who's going to pay for all that feed you scarf up like there's no tomorrow?"

Prince let her rub his velvety nuzzle before throwing his head back out of reach. She laughed, knowing this was his way of telling her he understood but didn't like it.

Working with Khalid was no chore, and Livy was careful not to show her eagerness in front of Prince as she returned him to his stall. Khalid was amazingly beautiful, a quick learner, and she loved the Arabian colt as if he were her own.

He greeted her with youthful enthusiasm as soon as she approached him, shifting between his two front hooves, nodding his head, knowing he'd make her laugh.

"Come on, you little ham." She led him outside and he strained against the lead, anxious to get started with his lesson. He seemed a little more spirited than usual and she had to calm him down several times during their session.

After leading him around the third time, she understood why Khalid was so animated. He loved audiences and two people stood on the southern slope watching them. Startled, Livy wondered how long they'd been standing there, and when she didn't resume training, the pair started down the slope toward her and Khalid.

The men didn't walk side by side, the one with the dark full beard lagged several feet behind. He was wearing the type of clothing the Colemans wore when showing Arabians.

She tugged the rim of her hat down to cut the sun's glare and squinted for a better look at the man in front of him. He was taller, broader, his hair black and shiny, and he had on some kind of brown silk shirt. Not the usual ranch garb.

She knew the Colemans were expecting company, but when the other hands were speculating at breakfast that royalty was coming to visit, she'd thought it was a bunch of hogwash. Of course everyone knew that Alex, Mac and Cade were descendants of some Arab sheikh...as hard as that was to believe. She knew that Cade's wife, Serena, was from the mid-East and that her father had visited once. But she didn't think any more of those people would be coming here.

Khalid whinnied and she absently patted his neck, helplessly fascinated by the approaching stranger. He sure walked as if he owned the place.

The instant he was close enough that she could see his face, Livy knew he had to be royalty. Her mouth knew it judging by the way it got drier than withered cotton. And trying to keep her heart from pounding through her chest was like nailing pudding to a tree. He was downright beautiful. Just like one of those princes in the fairy tales.

And he was coming straight toward her.

Should she bow? Curtsy? Heck, her knees were so weak she'd be lucky not to fall on her fanny.

About twelve feet away he stopped, and so did Livy's heart.

Every fairy tale she'd ever read flitted through her head.

He waved the man behind him forward. "Bring the

servant boy to me,'' he commanded in lightly accented English.

Livy blinked. Boy? Was Mickey trying to sneak up on her? She shot a look over her shoulder. Not a soul was in sight. Her attention immediately returned to the handsome stranger. He was looking directly at her.

She blinked again. He thought she was a—of all the damn nerve.

''My master summons you.''

She jumped at the gruff, heavily accented voice so close to her ear. Tilting her head back, she peered up into the dark face of the bearded man and scowled. ''Your what?''

The man frowned down at her, confusion taking the edge off his barbarous look. He hesitated, glanced at the other man, then said, ''You will come.''

She had a good mind to knock the turban off his head just as she'd done to Mickey's Stetson. Although this contraption would be more of a challenge. And then again, playing along could be a heck of a lot more fun.

She paused a moment longer, pulling her hat rim down lower, while trying not to look at the tall, handsome man waiting for her. Of course his high-and-mighty attitude had taken a bite out of his appeal.

''Come on, Khalid,'' she said, in as deep a voice as she could muster. ''Let's go see what this guy wants.''

He was only a few yards away and it was ridiculous to have to walk to him, but she did, leading Khalid in spite of his noisy protests. When Khalid halfheartedly reared, she whispered a few soothing words and he immediately calmed down.

Assured he would behave, she looked quizzically at the stranger, but he had eyes only for Khalid. Incredibly beautiful eyes. So dark blue they almost looked black. But it was the admiration she saw in them that warmed her heart. The man looked at Khalid as if he were the most magnificent horse in the world. Which Khalid was. Next to Prince, of course.

The man lifted his hand, and Livy stroked Khalid's side, letting him know it was okay to allow the stranger to touch him. The bearded man had immediately stepped several paces back, and while the other man checked Khalid's teeth, Livy freely studied the strong jut of his jaw, the deep cleft that dented his clean-shaven chin.

He had to be the sheikh. Except he was awfully young. About thirty, she guessed. Maybe he was the sheikh's son.

Whoever he was, he was gorgeous. Even if he was a snob and didn't have enough smarts to tell a male from a female.

She slowly glanced down at her worn jeans, the old plaid shirt Mickey had outgrown and passed on to her. It was really too big, but it was free, and with the enormous amount of oats Prince ate, she couldn't waste money on clothes.

She sighed. Okay, so maybe mistaking her for a boy wasn't so farfetched. Although she didn't suppose taking off her ragged hat would help. Not with the last haircut Mickey had given her.

"This animal, he was sired here?"

Animal? Livy bristled. Technically maybe. "Khalid is a fine Arabian colt."

Her snippy tone briefly drew his attention and she lowered her gaze, letting her hat shield her face as he stared down at her in silence. Finally he asked, "And the other one, the black gelding. How much are these animals?''

Her chin jerked up. "Neither one is for sale."

Their eyes met and his gaze immediately narrowed. She looked away and focused on stroking Khalid's neck, her heart pounding. What she said was true. Prince was safe. She wouldn't sell him for all the money in the world. And although the Desert Rose owners, Randy and Vi Coleman, had no intention of selling Khalid, if this guy was someone important, they might feel obligated to part with the foal.

Livy could barely stand the thought. "I have to take him in now," she mumbled, and started to turn, tugging on Khalid's lead.

The bearded man gasped and moved toward them, and she knew she'd made one of those faux pas things Rose had explained to her. But the sheikh guy, his gaze fastened stonily on her, raised a hand, and the other man stopped dead in his tracks.

Mr. High-and-Mighty probably expected her to stop, too. Tough. She led Khalid back into the stables, her heart rate not yet back to normal. Tempted to glance back, she looked straight ahead until they neared his stall. Then out of the corner of her eye, she noticed they had been followed inside. By the head honcho himself. The bearded man was nowhere to be seen.

She was going to ignore him, but when she started to open the gate, he reached out and held it closed.

"In my country, do you know how we handle such insolence from servants?" His voice was deep and close and annoyingly unnerving.

Itching to tell him she didn't give a hoot, Livy carefully kept her eyes lowered and her mouth clamped shut. No matter what a pain this guy was, he was a guest of the Colemans, and as much as it irked her, she supposed she ought to hold her tongue.

"Do you know who I am, boy? I warn you. Do not ignore me."

That did it. Livy may have to behave, but Khalid was, after all, *just an animal.* She whispered something in the horse's ear and he suddenly threw up his head, catching the man off guard. Before he could recover, Khalid nudged him hard enough that he stumbled forward.

Struggling for balance, he reached out, groping for a pole. And got a handful of Livy's right breast.

His eyes widened in shock as they met hers, and he curled his fingers, filling his palm more fully, almost in disbelief.

Livy yelped, and shoved him away from her.

His Royal Highness landed on his royal heinie.

Chapter Two

A woman!

Stunned, Sharif propped himself up on one elbow. He should have known, should have sensed somehow that this wisp of a female was not a boy. Without having her soft feminine flesh fill his palm.

He was reminded of her unexpected warmth as he stared up into striking violet eyes. Bewitching eyes that flooded him with wariness.

Laughing eyes.

He straightened, aware suddenly of the undignified way he lay sprawled on the ground. Hay fell from his hair. Mud splattered the front of his shirt, making the fabric cling to his skin.

Sharif sniffed and cursed. There was more than mud ruining the expensive silk.

"If you're waiting for an apology, you'll be sitting there for one heck of a long time." She stuck out her hand, and when he scowled, she shrugged and backed up. "Suit yourself."

Slowly he started to raise himself. Arms folded across her chest, head cocked slightly to the side, she watched him, looking more amused than alarmed when he finally got to his feet and towered nearly a foot over her.

"Do you know who I am?" he asked in a deceptively calm voice.

She paused with a considering expression, then shrugged. "Not exactly." At her indifference, his anger grew. "Want me to call your flunky?"

He frowned at the unfamiliar word.

"Your servant?" Her eyes widened in innocence, mocked by her tone. "Or can you handle this by yourself?"

The violet color was extraordinary, but her mouth was tarter than a lemon. He wondered what shade her hair was, all tucked under that hat. Wisps of light brown stuck out here and there, and an occasional blond strand. He could order her to remove the ugly tan hat. He doubted she would obey.

That anyone would dare oppose him was a staggering thought. And a woman? Almost unthinkable. But of course, this was America, a country of strange customs.

"Why do you pose yourself as a boy?" Sharif asked as he begun unbuttoning his shirt.

Her gaze settled on his right hand, turning increasingly wary with each button he unfastened. Apprehension darkened her eyes and gave him enormous satisfaction. Without the smug look she was even prettier.

"For your information, lots of girls dress like this here. We don't go prancing around in stuff that looks like night clothes and flimsy veils for your benefit." She briefly looked from his hand to his face and back again. "What are you doing?"

"Ah, so you do know who I am and where I come from." He shrugged off the shirt.

She took a step back. "I don't know who you are." Her gaze leveled on his bare chest, and she blinked. "What are you, some kind of sheikh or prince?"

He tossed the shirt over the side of the stall, mostly to distance himself from the slight odor, and advanced toward her.

She ducked behind the horse. "We have laws here, you know. Just because you're some sheikh, or whatever, you can't just do what you want."

He moved around to the front of the horse.

She scurried toward its left flank. "You don't intimidate me, so don't even try."

He stopped and focused on the horse, virtually ignoring her except to ask, "What is this animal's name?"

"Quit calling him an animal. This is Khalid."

Sharif nearly smiled at the relief she could not keep from softening her voice. And when she stepped around to reverently stroke Khalid's side, Sharif felt a swell of admiration edging out his irritation with her. In his experience, women seldom found animals so captivating.

"And I bet he comes from more royal stock than you do," she added with a sidelong glance that did not make it higher than his chest.

Her obvious appreciation of him should have inspired satisfaction, but her remark stung. All his life he had known exactly who he was. Or thought he had. In minutes everything had changed. His mother was American. Rich but not of royal blood.

He did not want to think about this dilemma now. He had come looking for distraction. His gaze drew back to the woman. "And you? What are you called?"

"Olivia Smith." She lifted her chin. "You may call me Ms. Smith."

A smile breached Sharif's lips. She was a most unusual woman. "Well, Ms. Smith, tell me about Khalid."

She gave him a sour look and mumbled, "Livy. Everyone calls me Livy." Adjusting her hat, she turned to remove the horse's bit. More light brown strands floated around her face. Chopped, uneven strands. He detested short hair on women. Another American and European custom with which he did not agree.

"In this country, when someone tells you their name you're supposed to return the favor," she said, her attention entirely focused on removing Khalid's bridle.

Sharif hesitated, unfamiliar with her phrasing. Having been educated in London, he had excellent command of the English language, but this woman bewildered him. In many ways.

She continued to concentrate on Khalid, unbuckling the throatlatch and noseband with a firm but loving hand even though Sharif could tell she was annoyed with him. Another puzzle. In his country, even in London and Monte Carlo, women sought him out. Beautiful women. Accomplished women. They strove to please him in every way.

He thought again about what she had said. *Return the favor.* "I am Sharif Asad Al Farid," he said proudly, guessing, not wishing to ask her to explain.

She wrinkled her nose at him. "Huh?"

He grunted his impatience. Did she really not know who he was? Back in his country, the entire palace staff would have been advised of an important arrival. Of course King Zak and Rose were concerned about reporters. Sharif himself was not anxious to be their prey as he had been in the past.

"That's a whole lot of names. What am I supposed to call you?" She looked utterly perplexed. And charming. "And don't say, Your Royal Highness. That's too big a mouthful...besides being weird."

"Then just Your Highness will do fine." The teasing words left his lips before Sharif realized he had the capacity to jest. The result was pleasing, however, when Livy stared at him in openmouthed surprise.

She had a fine mouth. Straight white teeth, lush pink lips that needed no artificial color. Lips that suddenly curved.

"I thought you were serious for a minute," she said, "until I saw that little twinkle in your eye."

His good humor fled and he straightened. "My eyes do not *twinkle.*"

"Sure they do." She slowly eased the bit out of Khalid's mouth, then stopped to study Sharif a moment. "But right now you look like a mean old grizzly bear. You really ought to smile and twinkle more. You look so much more handsome. Of course you already know how beautiful you are."

Her frank, unguarded expression startled him almost as much as her heartfelt words. Judging by the pink color seeping into her cheeks, they had surprised her, as well. Quickly she averted her gaze and tended to the tack, her movements slightly awkward.

Since he was a child he had been lavished with compliments and flattery, but none he could remember that affected him more. Her earnestness touched a place deep inside him, buried beneath the artifice privilege and wealth often fostered. Unlike many others, she did not use her honeyed words to curry favor. She spoke impulsively with the openness of a child.

After she made sure Khalid was secure in his stall, she eyed the barn door. She was about to flee, Sharif was sure of it, but he did not want her to go. When she made a sudden move, he reached for her arm. It was so small and fragile, he immediately loosened his grip, afraid he would hurt her.

"What in the Sam Hill do you think you're doing?"

She tried to twist out of his grasp, but she was no match for him.

"I do not intend to hurt you. I only want—" Sharif stared into her anxious eyes. What did he want? To erase the past week when his entire life had changed? This girl could not help him. No one could. His demons were his alone to battle. "I want you to take off your hat."

"Excuse me?"

He raised his free hand to accomplish the task himself, but she ducked away. "It is you who are beautiful. You should not dress like a boy."

"I'm not dressed like a—" She stopped, her eyes narrowing. "What did you say?" Anger tinged her voice and she stared at him as though he were the devil himself.

Her unexpected reaction caught him off guard, so when she jerked away, he lost his grip and she used her freed hand to jam her hat more securely on her head. "Never mind. Don't you dare repeat it," she said, her voice breaking. "That was low, really low. Even for someone like *you*."

"Wait." He blocked her path, then when she tried to get around him, he held her by the shoulders. "I do not understand."

"I know I don't act or look like other girls, but I don't need you pointing it out, buster." She jabbed a finger in his chest. "And for your information, not every girl *wants* to be beautiful. I'm fine just the way I am."

He fisted a hand around hers before she jabbed him again. Her nails were short, but they were ragged and chafed his skin. She tensed under his touch. "I will not hurt you," he repeated.

"You already have," she muttered, and he promptly released her. "I have to get back to work." She briefly glanced over her shoulder. "I can clean your shirt, if you want. I feel partly responsible."

He waved a dismissive hand. He had many more like them. "I want to understand why I have angered you. In my country, women like to be told they are beautiful."

She sighed. "Here, they like to be told the truth." One side of her mouth lifted. "Most of them." She shrugged. "Okay, most of the time we do."

She sighed again and looked at him with an odd longing in her eyes. This was not a woman who tried to hide her feelings. A new experience for him that was both refreshing and unsettling.

"Olivia Smith, take off your hat." She scowled at his command, and he grudgingly added, "Please." Not a word he used often, it rolled gruffly off his tongue.

She touched the rim uncertainly. "Why?"

"It hides your face and hair."

"That could be a good thing. Trust me."

"No." He slowly moved his hand toward the hat. "Trust me."

Livy froze, closing her eyes, barely able to breathe as he gently lifted the hat off her head. His movement was so smooth and unhurried, it seemed sensual some-how, and for one glorious moment, she did feel beau-tiful and feminine. Which was ridiculous, except Livy never wasted the opportunity for a good fantasy. She wondered if this was the way Cinderella had felt when her prince slipped on the glass slipper.

Of course a gorgeous, sparkling glass slipper was a far cry from a stained secondhand Stetson. Reluctantly she opened her eyes, forcing herself to give up the brief daydream.

His smile stole her breath again. Her chest tightened until it hurt. And then she saw her hand, as though it were no longer a part of her body, lying against his bare skin, his hardening nipple pressing into the center of her palm.

She gasped, snatched her hand back and squeezed her eyes shut tight. Humiliation burned in her cheeks. How had this happened? How had she gotten so carried away? How could she ever look at him again?

She couldn't. That's all there was to it. Taking a blind step back, she felt around for her hat, ready to yank it out of his hand and run. She found a belt buckle instead. And it wasn't hers.

"Oh, my God." Her eyes flew open and she pulled back her hand as if she'd just touched a red-hot burner. "I didn't mean to do that. I—I—" The heck with the hat. She started to turn to sprint for the door.

He stopped her with a firm hand. "Stay."

"Not a chance."

He hooked a finger under her chin and, when she tried to jerk away, he forced her head up. She closed her eyes and refused to meet the dark, steely blue of his gaze. If he laughed at her, sheikh or no sheikh, she'd slug him. She swore she would.

Warm breath tickled her cheek and her lids involuntarily lifted. "What are you doing?"

He lowered his mouth to hers and pressed a gentle kiss against her lips. When he pulled back, her throat closed at the look she saw in his eyes. She'd never seen a man look like that before, his pupils dilated so much that his eyes looked more black than blue. Maybe in the movies she'd seen it, but not in person, and certainly not directed at her. It made her feel all funny and squishy inside.

When his hold on her arm tightened she should have been frightened, but she was too fascinated by the way his jaw clenched, like Mickey's did when he was really angry or excited and was trying to hold back from popping someone or doing something crazy. But this man wasn't angry. He was...

She wasn't quite sure what, but just watching him look at her made her embarrassingly damp in a place she didn't expect.

"I didn't say you could kiss me," she said without the slightest hint of conviction, and wondered what it would take for him to do it again. She'd only kissed three boys before today, and none of those times seemed to count anymore.

His mouth lifted in a slight curve. "Had I asked, what would you have said?"

"No way."

"May I kiss you again?"

"Okay."

His smile broadened a little and Livy swallowed, not sure what she should do. Was she supposed to pucker up, or wait until he lowered his head again? Was it all right to lay her hand on his chest? She liked the feel of his smooth taut skin, and figured if she was going to let him kiss her again, what difference did it make where her hand landed.

He relieved her of the decision by placing her arms around his neck. Her breasts flattened against him and her head got a little fuzzy. The sudden shocking wish that they were bare skin to bare skin sobered her a little and she stiffened.

Stroking her back, he whispered something in a strange language. When she tilted her head back to look at him, he said, "You have the most magnificent eyes."

And then his gaze fell to her lips and she didn't think she'd ever wanted anyone to kiss her more than she did at this very moment. A few feet away Khalid whinnied, and she vaguely recalled where she was, that she was supposed to be working, that Mickey or any of the others could walk in at any time. But she just couldn't pull herself away.

This was her dream come to life—a handsome Prince Charming, words and looks that made her feel wanted and beautiful, and her need was so great, she brazenly stretched up to meet her fantasy.

His lips weren't so gentle this time. Her breath caught at the almost savage way he crushed her to him, as though he were being driven by some unknown force. The intensity both frightened and thrilled her. It was like something out of the movies, or in those romance books she sometimes read.

When his tongue slid along the seam of her lips, slowly applying pressure, looking for entry, she tensed again. Long enough for sanity to surface, and she pulled her arms from around his neck and shoved him back.

He looked dazed for a moment, and then he frowned. "You did not want my kiss?"

She rubbed her arms. "I'm not sure." She did, and she didn't. Mostly it was her own reaction that upset her. But the look of shock on his face eased her tension and she chuckled.

"Don't take it personally. It's just that I'm not very—" She clamped her mouth shut. The truth about her lack of experience was far more than he needed to know.

"I think I'd better go get that stain out of your shirt." She turned to leave, but stopped when he touched her hair.

Her hair!

Flattening her palms against her scalp, she groaned. She knew darn well how her hair looked after removing her hat. What in the world was she thinking?

She wasn't thinking. That was the problem. This man had her all tied up in knots. She liked living and working at the Desert Rose. Finally she'd found a place where she felt she belonged, where she was truly one of the team. But if anyone walked in and found them, in a second it could all be over.

Before she knew what was happening, he pulled her hands away from her head. "Why do you hide?" he asked, rubbing some strands of hair between his fingers. "Your hair is the color of honey. It could be very beautiful."

She didn't miss the "could be." In a last-ditch effort not to look like a total hag, she fluffed out her bangs, ran her fingers through the crown as she took a couple of steps back.

"I still don't know what to call you," she mumbled. He stared at her in that intense way she found so fascinating. As if no one else existed in the entire state of Texas. "Sharif."

"Is that your first name?"

He nodded and reached for her hair again.

She ducked and patted it down. What in the heck did he find so interesting about a ratty clump of squashed hair? Given the chance, she'd trade her new pocketknife for a mirror about now. "Does everyone call you Sharif? Or do you have a nickname?"

He frowned and absently scratched his chest, a movement she found so ridiculously exciting that she had to take a deep breath. "Why do you Americans have this obsession with nicknames? Is it not enough to be called the name given you by your mother?"

She made a face. "Sometimes a shorter name sounds more friendly, I suppose."

"Your mother, did she call you Livy?"

"I don't have a mother."

His eyebrows drew together. "Everyone has a mother."

"Not if she gives you away." Livy blinked at how pathetic she sounded. She really hadn't meant to, she was more concerned with the way he was inching closer again. But her words stopped him.

"And your father?"

"I have to get back to work now." She rubbed her palms down the front of her jeans and moved toward the door.

"Olivia? Your hat."

The way he said her name with a slight accent made her shiver, and she seriously thought about forgetting the Stetson. Especially when she turned around and saw the play of muscles across his tanned back as he bent to pick it up.

"Uh, thanks." She tried to grab the hat when he held it up to her, but he kept it a few inches out of reach. "That isn't very gentlemanly."

His eyebrows rose in phony surprise. "Did I claim to be a gentleman?" Smugness lifted his lips in a half smile. "One kiss, for one hat."

"Talk about obsessions. What's with you and kissing?"

"Ah, you do not like the sport."

Her mouth dropped open. "Sport?" She threw up her hands. "That's the problem with guys like you. You think...you think...kissing is a...is a sport. No thanks."

Great. Now she was a liar *and* unoriginal. Because, despite her words to the contrary, she very much wanted him to kiss her again. She wanted to feel breathless, and get that squishy feeling again that made her insides turn into Jell-O.

"We have known each other for only twenty minutes." He slid the rim of her hat between two fingers in an unhurried, annoying fashion. "What would you call it?"

The truth stung. She held out her hand. "Give me the hat."

He smiled. "I had forgotten how interesting you Americans can be. In my country, the women do not play these games."

"Do they have a choice?"

His expression tightened. "How much do you know about my country? Are you that wise in other cultures?"

Livy grimaced. Apart from the fact she had no idea where Sharif was actually from, she sure as heck didn't know much about geography or other countries, period.

She'd only squeaked her way through school because Father Mike would have tarred and feathered her if she hadn't. Riding horses had been a much preferable pastime.

Remembering how his servant dressed like something out of the movies, she said, "I bet you have a harem."

His eyes darkened, and his voice was low and edgy. "I force no one. Women come to me freely."

"You *do* have a harem?" She'd spoken impulsively, not truly believing such a thing existed, but from the look on his face... "Holy cow! You are something else."

"And you have a very vivid imagination."

"Which is about to leak out without my hat on. Hand it over."

"You know the terms." He dangled it just out of reach.

"I thought you didn't have to force women."

"Do you truly feel coerced?" He was looking at her like that again, studying her face with an eerie single-mindedness, lingering on her lips as if she was some kind of dessert.

And like a darn fool, her entire body was getting all feeble again. "I think I'll call you Shay. I went to school with a kid named Shay and he was a royal pain, too." She chuckled at her little joke. He didn't. "It's close enough to Sharif."

Just as she'd hoped, he forgot all about the hat and scowled at her. "I forbid you to call me by that name."

"Really?" She jumped up and snatched the Stetson out of his hand. "Thank you very much," she said with a sarcastic grin, while walking backward away from him. "Shay."

If she'd only kept the taunt to herself she probably could have made it out of the barn. But her hesitation allowed him to lunge forward and grab her around the waist. She dropped the hat, lost her footing and they both tumbled to the ground.

She scrambled to keep from being pinned beneath him, but she wasn't quick enough. "Get off. You're squashing the life out of my windpipe."

That wasn't all. Her breasts were crushed against his shoulder, and the really scary part was she kind of liked it.

He eased up, and just when she thought he was going to let her go, he repositioned himself, straddling her, keeping her back flat to the ground. His fingers locked around her wrists as he stared down at her with a triumphant smile.

"What did you call me?" The slight cocky lift of his left eyebrow made her see red.

She glared back at him, weighing the use of a threat against indifference. Except she was far too aware of the strength in his thighs pressing against her hips, and she couldn't think all that straight.

"This is very undignified, *Your Highness,*" she finally said, and was pleased to see his jaw clench.

"True," he said, with a slight shift of his hips. "But quite pleasant."

Boy, howdy. She swallowed. This was so unreal. Not a blessed guy she knew would ever think of manhandling her this way. "Aren't you afraid your flunky will come in here and find you bullying me?"

"If you really wanted to end this, you would simply call me Sharif."

The truth brought a wave of realization and shame

that made Livy's cheeks burn. "Sharif," she quickly murmured.

But it was too late. He knew she'd enjoyed his attention, the brief taboo run on the wild side. His expression didn't show it, though, and for that she was grateful.

As soon as she started to move, he got off. When he offered a hand, she took it. He pulled her to her feet but didn't immediately let her go. His gaze holding hers, he touched her shoulder. His warm fingertips met with bare skin.

She realized then that she'd lost a button and her too-big shirt had slid off her shoulder. He surprised her by gently pulling the fabric in place. Then he kissed her.

Just as her stubborn shirt slipped down again, a flash went off at the barn door.

Chapter Three

Sharif turned in time to see the back of the man's blue jacket and blond hair as he fled the barn. It took Sharif a moment to realize what had just happened. Even though he should have smelled the damn reporter from a hundred yards away, vile creatures that they all were.

Without even a glance at Livy, he ran after the man, but he was too late. All he caught was a glimpse of a speeding dark sedan, creating so much dust it was hard to see anything at all.

He swore loudly when he remembered he had no shirt. What a picture that would make. His father would not be pleased. Rose's feelings, Sharif did not care about.

Looking back toward the barn, he saw no sign of the woman. Olivia. With the big innocent violet eyes. He let out a heavy sigh and shoved a hand through his hair. Hay flew everywhere. He swore again.

For a moment he thought about returning to her. She had been a most pleasant distraction from his maddening thoughts. That she was a timid partner did not bother him. In fact, the new experience had been stimulating. Her uncertainty had barely masked her eagerness to explore, a naiveté he found enchanting.

She was young, barely twenty he guessed. Perhaps she had not yet been with a man. Although in his experience with American and European women, youth meant little in terms of sexual enlightenment.

He would run into Olivia Smith with the bewitching violet eyes again, he was sure of it. But for now, his thoughts were tainted with the intrusion of the reporter, and the possible repercussions of a suggestive photograph.

Sharif frowned when he realized what little regard he had given such offenses in the past. And much to the displeasure of his parents, there had been a considerable number of compromising situations that had provided fodder for the tabloids. What was different now? Was maturity finally replacing his childish antics?

As much as he wanted to believe age and wisdom were responsible, deep down Sharif knew better. Life was no longer so simple. The entitlement and privilege, the very foundation of his being he had taken for granted a mere two weeks ago were more precarious today. And Sharif wished more than anything he had been kept in ignorance. Because for the first time in his life, he understood fear.

HALF THE MORNING HAD GONE by before Livy got up the nerve to return Shay's shirt. She seldom had reason to go to the main house and everyone would wonder what the heck she was doing there. Maybe she ought to just leave the darn thing in the barn, and Shay could let his servant fetch it.

If she were smart that's exactly what she would do, she told herself as she marched up the slope toward the house. So far, no one had given her any funny looks that said they knew what had happened in the barn yesterday. She still cringed every time one of the other hands so much as looked her way, though, half expecting them to make some remark. But she supposed it was her own guilty conscience acting up.

And why shouldn't it, with the racy dreams she'd had last night. She could've sworn she was having one of those hot flashes she'd heard about. Now, just thinking about her and Shay rolling around in their skivvies in her dream brought on a heat wave, and she stopped to mop her forehead.

The last thing she wanted to do was get all hot and sweaty by the time she got to the house. Not that it should matter. Working outside under the hot sun, she could get pretty ripe by eleven most mornings. And that was with her hat on. Today she'd left it off. Even under the best circumstances her hair looked like someone had used a mixing bowl to cut it. There was no need to let it get all stuck to her head. After all, she *was* going to the main house.

Who was she kidding?

Grunting in disgust, she jammed her hat on her head and hurried up the slope. By the time she arrived at the kitchen door, the silk shirt she had carefully ironed was a crumpled mess.

Through the screen she saw Ella Grover sitting at the kitchen table, her head bowed. Livy frowned at the confusing picture. The spry cook was always bustling around the stove. But it was Vi Coleman who was stirring something in a skillet. She jerked and turned at Livy's knock, her red hair in disarray around her face.

"Livy! Am I glad to see you. Come on in." Mrs. Coleman sighed, then sent a stern look toward Ella when the older woman started to rise. "Sit. Livy will refill your water." Mrs. Coleman turned beseeching green eyes toward Livy. "Do you mind?"

"Of course not." Livy cast the shirt aside and hurried to the table for the empty glass. "What's wrong, Ella? You sick?"

"No," the woman said, and scowled at her boss.

"Ouch!" Vi Coleman jerked her hand away from the skillet handle. "Gosh darn it."

"I told you to use a pot holder with that one," Ella said, and started to rise again.

"Ella Grover, if you don't stay in that chair, so help me, I'll have Randy carry you to your room."

At the mention of Mr. Coleman, the cook snorted. "Ain't nobody going to lift this body and live."

Livy hid a grin as she returned the filled glass to the table. Ella and her husband Hal had been with the Colemans for so many years they were more like family than employees. That's what Livy liked most about living and working on the Desert Rose. The Colemans never treated anyone like an outsider. Not even her.

"Can I help you with something, Mrs. Coleman?" she asked, her gaze sweeping the cluttered counters and food spills. It was weird to see the kitchen like this. Ella usually kept it so spotless.

"I'd sure appreciate it. Ella had a dizzy spell and I don't want to call Abbie for help what with the baby due so soon." She pulled a red gingham oven mitt out of the drawer. "But you've got to start calling me Vi." Mrs. Coleman smiled. "For goodness' sakes, you've worked here for over fours years now. You're practically family."

Family. A lump blocked Livy's throat and she couldn't swallow. She blinked just in case her eyes got any strange ideas about tearing up. All she had ever wanted was to find a place to belong. She never dreamed she could be so lucky. "Okay...Vi." She cleared her throat. "I'm not much of a cook, but if you tell me what to do, I'm sure we can get lunch on the table in no time."

Vi and Ella exchanged bland looks. "Breakfast," Vi said.

Livy looked at the oak-carved wall clock. Everyone at the ranch should have been up and at 'em hours ago.

"Don't ask." Vi pushed stray hair away from her shiny damp face and opened the oven. The aroma of biscuits filled the kitchen.

"She don't have to ask." Ella snorted, and inclined her head toward the tray of biscuits Vi removed. "And if you think *he's* gonna be content with such *peasant* food, you're kidding yourself."

Livy's eyes widened. Shay. She should have known.

"Come on, Ella, he's from a different culture, and he is the boys' brother. Besides, he won't be here long. It won't hurt to be nice to him." Vi's gaze darted to Livy. "So we all smile, okay?"

"Don't worry." Livy shrugged, and turning to grab an apron, muttered, "I've already met his royal pain in the butt."

Vi's gasp told her she'd spoken too loudly. Ella chuckled.

Heat climbed Livy's neck. "I'm sorry. He's your guest and I shouldn't have said that."

Vi shook her head and turned to lift the biscuits off the baking sheets. But not before Livy saw her check a grin. "Get the butter out of the refrigerator, will you?"

Livy breathed with relief and did as she was asked. "How about the cream?"

"It probably isn't thick or sweet enough for him."

"Ella." Vi's voice was strained. "Please."

The cook gave Livy a quick look then stared down at her hands. No one said anything after that. Vi finished arranging the biscuits on a red cloth napkin lining a basket, and Livy stacked some plates to be taken into the dining room.

Vi was usually the most pleasant, even-tempered person Livy had ever met. But not lately. Her mood could sink lower than the hundred-year-old well out back. There was lots of speculation around the ranch about what was happening. Everyone loved her and they were all concerned.

Personally, Livy figured Vi's moodiness had to do with all the attention her husband was paying one of the boarders. Her name was Savannah and she was one of those gals who always had on just the right clothes and makeup. Still, Livy didn't think it was anything to worry about. She'd be a mighty happy woman if she had a husband like Randy Coleman looking at her the way he looked at Vi.

Ella made a tsking noise with her tongue. "You gonna stand there woolgatherin', or help Vi?"

Livy gave the older woman a cheeky grin. "Good thing you're such a good cook, because you sure are bossy."

Ella tried to snap a dish towel across Livy's fanny, but Livy was too quick and scooted out of the way. "Tell that to His Highness in there." Ella inclined her head toward the dining room. "He already turned down my blueberry pancakes."

Livy stopped two feet from the dining room door. Panic fluttered in her belly. He was in there? Already?

She thought he was upstairs waiting to be called down. She wasn't ready to face him yet.

"What's wrong, Livy? You look as pale as Ella." Vi put down the spatula and stared at her with concern. "I hope there isn't a bug going around."

Livy took a quick breath. "Nope. I'm fine. I was just…" She took another breath, this one deeper. "I was just wondering if I should take some coffee out there."

"Good idea. I made a fresh pot. Rose was going to come get it, but she must be catching up with her son."

Livy nodded absently, vaguely recalling that Shay was Rose's son and that they had only recently met. But it was hard to imagine an elegant, kind lady like Rose having an arrogant, fathead son like Shay.

After retrieving the coffeepot and patting her hair down, Livy pushed through the dining room door. She was tempted to pass by the antique mirror hanging over the corner buffet, but she decided she didn't give a fig about how she looked. Sort of.

His back was to her, his dark hair damp, probably from his shower. Of course, everyone else had been up for hours doing chores. She doubted he'd ever done a lick of work in his life.

Rose sat to his right, her blond hair held back in a youthful ponytail, making Livy wish she hadn't let Mickey whack hers off. Another place was set across from Rose, but there was no sign of anyone else.

When a floorboard creaked under Livy's boot, Rose looked up and smiled. "What a surprise to see you here," she said, and Livy tried not to wince. "Have you met my son?"

Shay didn't even bother to turn around to see who Rose was talking to. Livy briefly thought she could set

down the coffee and cream and get out before he saw
her. Especially after Rose's comment. He was going to
think Livy was here to see him. Which was mostly true,
but still...

A slight frown creased the older woman's brows,
and Livy realized she hadn't responded. Hadn't done
anything, in fact, but stare at the back of Shay's im-
mobile head. "Uh, yeah, we met," she mumbled, and
saw him straighten.

"Oh, really?" Rose smiled again, and looked from
Livy to Shay. "At the stables?"

An innocent question, a logical one, really, since
that's where Livy worked, but she stiffened with guilt
and Shay finally turned toward her. It was a slow, almost reluctant movement that set Livy's teeth clench-
ing. Just before she would have met his eyes, she
bowed her head to pour the coffee.

He didn't say anything, which did nothing to ease
Livy's nerves. Better the jackass didn't acknowledge
her, she told herself, but she couldn't do a darn thing
about the heat crawling up her neck and stinging her
cheeks.

"Livy? Are you all right?" Rose started to rise, but
Livy waved for her to stay seated.

"I'm fine. Ella's got some kind of bug, and Mrs.
Coleman asked me to help out, but it looks like I might
be coming down with something, too." The words
came out so fast and garbled that Livy wanted to sink
into the seams of the hardwood floor.

Against her will, her gaze met Shay's. Amusement
glittered in his dark blue eyes, but his expression never
wavered.

"The sugar needs replenishing," he said calmly, and
turned his attention away from her.

She blinked, stunned by his dismissal. His callous words dug their claws into her, and hurt replaced surprise. She moistened her suddenly dry lips and glanced at Rose.

The older woman was staring at her son with disapproval. She slowly lifted her napkin to her lips and dabbed a little, letting silence grow before she said, "King Zak is a lovely man. I'm sure he raised you with manners, Sharif."

Livy wanted to disappear. She looked helplessly at the coffee. Rose would probably understand if Livy left the pot on the table and hightailed it out of here. Of course, judging by the way Shay's jaw clenched, he just might beat her to the door. Right after he exploded.

But to her utter amazement, he did nothing. After a brief but awkward silence, he said, "I did not mean to be rude."

He didn't look at Livy or Rose, but faced straight ahead and that suited Livy just fine. Rose didn't seem too pleased by the vague apology, but she didn't push it.

"Your breakfast should be ready at any minute," Livy mumbled as she poured the coffee, her gaze carefully directed to the chore. "Is there anything else you need besides sugar?"

"I'll get it." Rose started to rise. "I told Vi I'd love to help."

"Oh, no. I'll get it." Livy jerked the pot and coffee sloshed over Shay's cup into the saucer and splattered his shirt cuff. "Oh, boy." She stared at the spray of brown against the snow-white silk. "Sorry." She hoped he'd brought a lot of shirts.

He barely moved. His accusing gaze went from the dotted cuff to Livy's face.

"It was an accident." She lifted her chin.

"Of course it was," Rose said, dipping her napkin in her water glass and reaching over to dab at the cuff.

Shay pulled away, and looked at Livy again. He said nothing as he extended his hand toward her, the soiled part of the cuff facing her.

Obviously he wanted her to clean it. She stared him down for a moment, tempted to pour the rest of the coffee over his head. But for Rose's sake, Livy forced a smile and set the pot aside.

"Sharif." Annoyance edged into Rose's voice.

"No problem," Livy said quickly, and plucked Shay's linen napkin off his lap. Before he knew what she was doing, she dipped the fabric into his water glass and blotted the cuff.

He stared in disbelief. First at his wrist, and then at her. "Are you mad?"

"Fuming, actually," she said, her temper overcoming her embarrassment. He had kissed her just yesterday, and now he was treating her as if he barely knew her. Or worse, as if she was his personal maid. What a jerk!

"Mad as in insane." He snatched the napkin out of her hand, and started rubbing at the coffee stains himself.

"Gee, I'm glad to see you can do something for yourself." Livy had almost forgotten Rose was in the room until she heard her stifle a laugh.

Shay was too busy rubbing with a vengeance to notice, and Livy slid the older woman an apologetic look.

Rose merely grinned. "Where did you say you two met?"

"The stables—" Livy started.

"I had the misfortune of—" Shay said at the same time, "meeting this impudent—"

"Enough."

Everyone turned at the sound of a man's commanding voice. But not before Shay slid her a cool look. And she sent him a resentful one back.

"Good morning, Zak." Rose smiled broadly. "You're just in time for breakfast."

"I have already eaten." His gaze stayed glued on Shay. "Nearly three hours ago."

"I see." Rose shot a nervous glance at her son, whose sullen expression hadn't changed. "Then have some coffee with us, won't you?"

Livy vaguely knew that was her cue to pour the man a cup, but she was too fascinated by him. He had to be a king or sheikh. Although he wore regular clothes, he was tall and broad and very dark and mysterious looking. It was easy to picture him on a throne inside a grand palace just like in the fairy tales. If she hadn't seen the kindness in his eyes she might even have been afraid.

Instead of embarrassed. After all, these people were guests. Royalty, in fact. And she was the hired help.

"Livy?" Rose placed a gentle hand on her arm, and Livy jumped. "This is King Zakariyya Al Farid of Balahar, Sharif's father. Zak, this is Olivia Smith."

Maybe she was supposed to curtsy or something. Unsure, she dragged her palm down the front of her jeans, then stuck out her hand.

He accepted it, amusement twinkling in his eyes, but instead of a handshake, he brought the back of her hand up to his lips and kissed it. "I am enchanted to meet you."

Livy's eyes nearly popped out of her head. For a

moment she felt so grown-up and important and horribly giddy. What the heck was she supposed to say now? She glanced at Rose for a clue. Nothing. Her gaze automatically went to Shay. He had an odd gleam in his eyes. He almost looked angry.

She swallowed and shuffled. "Me, too," she finally mumbled as she freed her hand. "Uh, do you want coffee?"

King Zak nodded and, ignoring the place setting opposite Rose, he pulled out the chair beside her. To Livy's surprise, a faint pink spread across the older woman's cheeks. Livy quickly looked at Shay. He'd noticed, too. He didn't look pleased.

Livy scooted around the table and got the cup and saucer, then filled it for King Zak. As she set it before him, she felt the weight of Shay's stare, and she cautiously looked his way.

His gaze moved down her body, lingering on her breasts, before rising to lock with hers. Was he thinking about their kiss, about the way he'd touched her? Had he thought about her at all last night? The same squishy feeling that had made a fool out of her yesterday threatened her balance. She quickly looked away...to find Rose and King Zak watching her with interest.

"I'll go see how the food is coming. Anybody need anything else?" Her unnaturally high voice made her spitting mad, but she forced a smile.

"I don't think so." Rose looked questioningly at King Zak, who shook his head.

Shay picked up his water glass and napkin and held them up to Livy. "You do intend to replace these."

It wasn't a question. More of a command, and Livy had a good mind to tell him what he could do with the glass. Sideways. "Of course," she said politely, and fumed all the way back to the kitchen.

To think she'd wasted a precious night's sleep on that jackass, she thought as she pitched the damp napkin and filled a fresh glass with the special bottled water Ella must have bought for the visitors. Although why anyone wouldn't want the best-tasting well water in all of Texas from out back was beyond Livy's understanding. Of course nothing seemed good enough for Shay. Especially not her.

"Anything wrong?" Vi asked.

She was so self-absorbed, Livy had almost forgotten Ella and Vi were in the kitchen. "Not a thing. Be right back."

She hurried away before she started either cussing or sniveling and opened the door with her hip, then marched into the dining room, the water in one hand, the coffeepot in the other.

Shay turned at the sound of her footfalls. "Ah, there is the girl now." He frowned at her loaded hands, then lifted one eyebrow. "The sugar?"

"Oh, silly me. How could I have forgotten?" She set the coffeepot on the corner of the table, lifted the clean napkin she had draped over her arm and laid it across Shay's lap. That he jumped slightly pleased her enormously.

When he glanced menacingly at her, she pursed her lips. "You know what, Shay? You may be a hotshot in your country, but you really don't know beans about women."

His stunned look was worth her humiliation. She started to leave, careful not to make eye contact with King Zak or Rose. "Oh, I almost forgot your water," she said, as she turned back to Shay and poured it over his head.

Chapter Four

Sharif cursed as the ice-cold water ran down his neck and spine. He jerked back and nearly toppled over. Rose stared at him with a hand over her mouth, shock widening her light blue eyes. His father remained expressionless.

Behind Sharif, the door swished closed. The coward had left.

"I don't know what happened. Livy is usually such a sweet, sweet girl," Rose began, waving helplessly. "I—I..."

His father lifted a silencing hand and Rose promptly obeyed. He looked directly at Sharif. "Do you know what provoked the woman?"

Sharif snatched the napkin off his lap before it absorbed any more water, and used it to dry his face. And to avoid his father's probing eyes. "Why would I know about this crazy person? She is nothing more than a..."

After an awkward silence his father asked, "A what?"

He could not finish his initial thought aloud. Sharif's reluctance had nothing to do with his father's stern tone or the warning issued in his disapproving eyes. It was the recollection of the hurt in Olivia's face that stopped him.

Shamed him.

Angered him.

Surely the vixen did not regard their playfulness yesterday as anything significant. He was merely passing the time, looking for a distraction. So what had prompted her outrageous behavior?

The hurt in her violet eyes echoed in his head.

To her mind, it was apparent he had done something wrong.

"Sharif?"

His father's voice was quieter now, not so stern, making Sharif fear his expression had given away his self-doubt. He straightened and silently met the king's eyes in subtle defiance.

"Tell me, Sharif. What do you think the woman's punishment should be?"

"Oh, please, I'll talk to her—" Rose began in a pleading tone, but again King Zak lifted a hand and again she fell silent.

Sharif stared at her subdued face, unnerved by the oddest desire to tell her to stand up to King Zak, to not be so docile.

Which was absurd. Women in his country, and where Rose once was queen, were taught subservience from an early age. Sharif liked it that way.

He turned to his father's expectant face. "I will deal with her myself."

"In what manner?"

Sharif saw the amusement lurking in the king's eyes, and anger seized him once more. He would not be made the fool. Throwing down his napkin, he stood, heedless of his chair scraping the hardwood floor as it flung back.

Before he could say anything, a loud noise coming from outside drew their attention. Angry shouts, the slamming of car doors, the blare of a horn all sounded from somewhere in front of the house. King Zak and Rose both left the table and hurried toward the living room for a look through the expansive glass windows.

Sharif followed close behind, knowing deep down his nightmare was coming true. He had lain awake half the night, planning a counterattack if reporters were to show up again. He had no doubt the man yesterday was from the media, looking to publicize the shame of Sharif's heritage. The problem was, he had no plan, no defense. He was, in fact, not the blood heir to the throne of Balahar.

"Oh, no." Rose was first to the window, the sudden slump in her shoulders foretelling. "Reporters."

Sharif looked away from the comforting hand his father pressed to her lower back, and stared out at the same dark sedan he had seen yesterday. Two men stood face-to-face with one of the ranch hands, all of them gesturing wildly.

"There's Alex," Rose said, straightening, a trace of pride in her voice. "He'll take care of it."

With a mixture of admiration, envy and relief, Sharif watched his eldest brother approach the men. Rose was right. Alex probably would take care of everything. From what Sharif had witnessed, he was the most sensible and responsible of the four brothers.

As soon as Alex joined the group, the shouting stopped. Moments later, the two strangers got in their car and left.

Alex stood watching until the car disappeared out

the front gate. Their other brother, Cade, rode up on a black gelding, then climbed down to confer with Alex and the ranch hand. All three men glanced toward the house, and tension cramped Sharif's shoulders.

Of course the commotion was about him. And, to a lesser degree, King Zak. And possibly Rose. Sharif had to face public scrutiny sooner or later.

Alex and Cade started toward the house while the third man led the gelding toward the barn. Rose sighed as she watched her two sons approach.

"I'm sure everything is fine," she said, smiling.

She did not have to say her reassurance was due to Alex, and Sharif experienced a sting of jealousy. Absurd. These people meant nothing to him. He did like Alex. He seemed to be a good man, and Sharif was grateful to him for banishing the reporters. At least for now.

In fact, he liked all three of his brothers, and he hoped in time, they would become friends. But Rose could never replace his mother.

He saw the pride shining in her eyes as she watched Alex, and Sharif felt empty suddenly. He had seen how they interacted, as though they had never been separated. As though she had been the one who had dried his boyish tears and sung him to sleep. Sharif did not understand.

Perhaps they had a special bond because Alex remembered her. He had been four when Rose was torn from them. Cade and Mac were barely three and had no memory of her. Sharif had been the only one who had gone with her. Until he had outgrown the inside of her belly.

Sharif stepped back from the window, away from Rose, shaken by the sudden realization that they did have a bond, no matter how much he wanted to deny it. But in his heart, Queen Nadirah would always be his mother. Even though she had been ripped too early from his life. Her death still pained him.

His gaze automatically drew to Rose. Had she felt the same razor's edge slicing through her body when he had been torn away from her?

Sharif pushed the crippling thought out of his mind. He could not afford sympathy or regret or any other emotional obstacle. Not now. His future was at stake.

His brothers neared the house just as Olivia walked outside, and they all stopped to talk. At the sight of her, Sharif's chest tightened, oddly not from anger, but from something else. Something strange, foreign... something that made the hair at the back of his neck stand. As though she were some kind of primal threat to him.

He dismissed the ridiculous notion. Standing next to Alex, she looked small and fragile, like a child's doll. She could not be much over five feet, and her wrists and hands were so tiny, Sharif had been concerned about hurting her yesterday. But she was no wilting desert flower. She had not cowered before anyone's wishes as Rose had done.

Admiration dented his annoyance as he watched her with his brothers. Alex gestured toward the barn, and Olivia straightened. Shaking her head, she stuffed her hands into her pockets, her shoulders rolling slightly forward before she backed away and headed toward the stables.

Sharif wondered if their exchange had anything to do with yesterday. Olivia had done nothing wrong, and if Alex was upset, Sharif would speak to him.

"If you want to go change your shirt, I'll get the

boys some coffee," Rose said as she headed toward the kitchen. "Then we can all sit down and find out what the ruckus was about."

Sharif had totally forgotten about his shirt and wet hair. And he had never before heard the word *ruckus,* but he figured he knew what it meant. His shirt would have to wait.

A moment after Rose disappeared, Cade pushed through the dining room door just ahead of Alex. They both eyed Sharif's wet soggy condition but said nothing as they took seats at the table.

"We have a problem." Cade pushed a hand through his dark hair, concern etching lines across his forehead as he looked from Sharif to King Zak. "A couple of reporters know you're here."

"Sharks always smell blood. I only wish we had had more time." King Zak sighed. "Your mother is—"

"Yeah, we saw her in the kitchen, but we haven't told her anything yet." Cade grunted in disgust. "I'd better call Rena and warn her before the vultures start knocking on our door."

"Do not worry. My daughter is used to dealing with the press," King Zak said. "But, yes, it would be wise to warn her."

"Go call your wife." Alex motioned with his chin. "I'll fill them in."

Sharif watched Cade head toward the hall, struck again by the staggering changes in all their lives. Cade was not only his newfound brother, but his marriage to Sharif's adopted sister, Serena, made Cade his brother-in-law, as well. Although Serena was no blood relation to Rose, as a member of the royal family of Balahar and as Cade's wife, she would also be affected by any press releases.

When Sharif turned back to his father and Alex, he immediately met his brother's eyes. They were dark and intense, full of questions or, perhaps, disapproval.

"We have to make a decision," Alex said. "They know you're here, and denying it will probably just make matters worse. I say we make a joint statement, telling them the truth."

Sharif snorted in disagreement. "Those jackals will not be content until they have sniffed out every hint of scandal. I say we tell them nothing."

"The sooner we give them a story, the sooner they'll quit digging. They've already exploited every detail about Cade, Mac and me being long-lost royalty. The rest is bound to come out anyway." Alex's gaze held steady. "I assume you don't have anything to hide."

Sharif stiffened. Of course he did not, but he did not care for his brother's tone. "You think the story of Rose's wrongful imprisonment at the hands of her own sister-in-law, or the secret of my heritage are not scandals?"

"*Our* mother was the victim. When the news does break, and it will, the only person who's going to look bad is good ol' Aunt Layla."

Sharif turned away. Alex did not understand. How could he? They shared the same blood, but they did not share the same culture. He was more American in beliefs and attitude. Alex could not know how it felt to suddenly have both the past and future shattered.

"King Zak? What's your position on this?"

Sharif stared out the window as he waited for his father to answer Alex. He did not have to look at the older man to know that he thoughtfully stroked his chin as he considered his answer. King Zak was the wisest man Sharif had ever known, and in the end, he would abide by his father's wishes.

"How much do these men know?" King Zak finally asked, just as Rose carried in a tray of coffee.

Alex hesitated a moment. "These are the same guys who broke the story about Mother being kept drugged in the sanitarium in Europe while Mac, Cade and I were sent here." He slid a look at Rose, and her lips curved in a reassuring smile. "And of course they covered Cade and Serena's wedding. Now, they know you two are here." Alex looked pointedly at Sharif. "And they claim that my dear brother is having an affair with one of our ranch hands. Absurd, isn't it?"

Everyone in the room turned toward Sharif. Disapproval and annoyance darkened his father's face, while confusion furrowed Rose's eyebrows. Cade had just returned, his grim expression focused on Sharif.

"An affair?" Sharif made a dismissive gesture with his hand. "I have been here only twenty-four hours and already they claim I am having an affair. This is why I see no point in supplying them with information."

Alex shrugged, his unwavering gaze a clear indication he did not completely believe Sharif. "By the same token, what we don't give them, they make up."

"What is it you suggest we tell them?" King Zak asked.

Alex looked at Rose. "This may not be easy."

She did not react. Her attention was focused on Sharif's wet shirt. When her gaze rose to meet his, Sharif saw comprehension dawn in her eyes. She knew about him and Olivia.

Guilt nudged him. Which was ridiculous. A couple of kisses did not constitute an affair. And Olivia had been a willing participant. He would not have acted, otherwise.

"Mother?" Alex frowned at her before his eyes again found Sharif.

"You're right, Alex." She abandoned the tray of coffee and sank into a chair. "Let's tell them what we know."

He nodded. "Okay, let's discuss the wording and who'll be the spokesman."

To Sharif's amazement, Rose leaned forward, and resting her elbows on the table, said, "I've been thinking about this, and I think we should go ahead and give them a brief, factual chronological list of events."

Everyone nodded, no one looking the least surprised at the assertiveness in her voice or the sudden strength in her face. Fascinated by this other side of her, Sharif remained silent.

"First, we tell them about Ibrahim's assassination." She paused at the mention of her husband, a brief sadness touching her face and finding a soft spot in Sharif's stubborn heart. "How it was Azzam's wife, Layla, who had arranged for my imprisonment. And Ibrahim's murder." She briefly closed her eyes. "I was wrong in accusing my husband's brother and trying to retaliate. This is my chance to set the record straight."

Silence descended. It had been a shocking and ugly thing to learn that a twisted, sick thirst for power had resulted in the death of a king, and the ruin of his family. So many casualties. So many lies.

Sharif stared at Rose with grudging respect. Thirty years in a sanitarium, drugged and separated from her children, while still grieving for her husband. Yet she had survived.

He noticed a small scar near her ear and had the

oddest urge to touch it. To touch her. To draw from her strength. He shoved his hands into his pockets and stepped back.

Rose cleared her throat. "We'll tell them how I had sent you boys to my brother Randy for safekeeping, how Layla had pretended to be a friend, but had me committed to the sanitarium, while sending word to Randy that I was dead." She looked directly at Sharif and smiled. "And that I was pregnant with this handsome little one."

Cade snorted, and Alex faked a cough.

Sharif blinked. The strangest feeling tugged at his insides. An odd jumble of panic and pleasure, uncertainty and excitement. He stared at the teasing grin on Cade's face. These were his brothers. And they were joking with him. Just like brothers did.

A lump formed in his throat and he wanted to flee. Back to Balahar where he was in control. Where he knew the name of every desert flower and the exact time the sun would set. Where he could ignore the overwhelming changes shattering his life.

"Do I not have a say in this matter?" he asked, and at his abrupt tone, Rose's smile faded.

Cade's teasing grin turned to a scowl, and he was about to speak, but Rose held up a hand.

"What is your objection, Sharif?" Her voice was calm, patient, and he felt a moment's regret. For what, he had no idea. But for some alien reason, he only knew he did not wish to displease her.

"What will you say about my parents?" He paused. "King Zak and Queen Nadirah."

The qualification was needless, and he suddenly felt small for adding it.

"The truth," Rose said without reaction. "That

when Layla took you to them, they trusted her and adopted you, not knowing who you were." She slowly shrugged her slim shoulders and briefly glanced at King Zak. "They did nothing wrong. Layla told them your mother was dead, so they gave you a home. I will be forever grateful that they raised you to be such a fine young man."

But they lied to me.

Sharif did not vocalize the thought. "I do not see the necessity of drawing my name into this."

"They already know you're here, remember?" Cade said dryly, clearly not in possession of his mother's patience. "Besides, whether you like it or not, you are a part of this family."

Of his three brothers, Sharif knew Cade the best. They had met several months ago when Cade had been sent to Balahar to marry Serena. At the time, they did not know they were brothers. Life had been much simpler then.

"Yes, however, it is not just for myself that I am concerned. We must also consider what is good for Balahar."

Everyone fell silent. He knew they would not challenge him in this area. They were too ignorant of his culture, of what should have been their culture.

Everyone except King Zak. "Sharif, explain yourself," he said, frowning. "Surely you do not imply your position is threatened. The people will accept you as king. You know it is their wish that you serve them."

Sharif quickly turned to look out the window before anyone could see the fear in his eyes. How could his father be so sure? What did the men whisper as they gathered on the hillside to herd their sheep home? Were they not shocked that he was not a true blood son of Balahar?

"Sharif?"

He turned back to King Zak. "You know best, Father," he said briskly. "I will accept your decision. Excuse me. I need to change my clothes."

"Sharif."

Ignoring his father's command, he left the dining room, but not before he saw Rose lay a restraining hand on King Zak's arm. Sharif both resented and welcomed her interference. He did not want to have a discussion with his father right now. About anything. He wanted to be left alone.

He started to peel off his wet shirt before he even got to his room. Or perhaps he needed another distraction. Olivia did not think he knew how to treat a woman. A smile began to curve his mouth. Perhaps he should prove her wrong.

Chapter Five

"What are you whining about? You're not the one who made a darn fool of yourself yesterday," Livy said, and Khalid brought his head up and down with a loud neigh.

She snorted. "You don't have to agree with me. A little sympathy would be nice."

He nudged her so hard she momentarily lost her footing. He didn't want to give her any comfort. He wanted sugar.

She laughed. "At least I always know where I stand with you." She reached into her pocket and gave him his treat. "Unlike some other Arabian-type males."

Khalid watched her as he chomped, his large liquid brown eyes full of understanding. He and Prince were the only two critters in the entire universe who truly understood her. They easily read her moods, knew everything there was to know about her and loved her anyway. What more could a girl ask for?

Livy led Khalid into the ring, then stopped to look at the house. From where she was, she could only get a side shot, but it was enough to see that the reporters hadn't returned. She hadn't really expected them to after Alex and Cade got through with them, but she sure wished she knew what they'd talked about. Especially after the strange look Cade had given her.

She had done as they asked and spread the word to the other hands to not talk to anyone from the press. But she'd almost rather have sat in the dentist chair. No telling how many shades of red and purple she'd turned, half expecting someone to make a crack about her playing kissy-face with that jackass.

Her gaze reluctantly drew toward the far end of the house where the second-floor balcony overlooked the courtyard. Around the second stone arch the guest rooms started, and she wondered which one belonged to Shay. Not that she had a single intention of visiting him there. El Paso would freeze over first.

Obviously impatient to begin his training, Khalid whinnied, and Livy tore her gaze away from the house.

She jumped when she realized why Khalid had reacted. "What are you doing here?"

Shay had come up from behind her and stood not four feet away, an annoying smile lifting one side of his mouth. "I did not know there are areas that are off-limits."

"Well, now you do," she mumbled, and turned to stroke Khalid's neck. It wasn't fair that Shay could look so downright beautiful even after she'd doused him with water. "I don't want any distractions while I'm training."

He moved in beside her and she nearly tripped over her own feet. But all he did was run his hand down Khalid's silky mane. And Khalid, the traitor, closed his eyes in equine bliss and pressed himself against Shay's palm.

"I understand." He had eyes only for Khalid, for

which she should have been grateful. "He is beautiful. I will watch quietly."

Livy hadn't been prepared for that response and let several silent minutes pass. His focus remained so intent on Khalid, as he ran his hands up both forelegs, that he seemed to forget she was standing there.

"Look, if you're expecting me to apologize for dumping the water on you I'm not gonna do it."

He stopped examining Khalid and looked at her, his lips beginning to curve. "I understand. You were simply looking for my attention."

She blinked. "What?"

"I apologize for ignoring you. I well understand a woman needs—"

She stomped her foot. "I was not trying to get your attention. I'm not even speaking to you."

"I—"

"And if you say you understand one more time, I'm gonna—" She stopped herself, fairly certain the Colemans wouldn't want her to threaten their guest with bodily harm. Especially after the incident in the dining room. Who knew how much trouble lay ahead of her for that tantrum.

She deliberately turned away from him. "I don't think you should be out here. You never know if the reporters will be back."

Shay remained silent long enough that she slid him a curious sideways glance. His jaw was clenched, and he turned back to Khalid. "My life will not be ruled by reporters."

"No, but they can make things awfully sticky."

He made a dismissive sound. "They make up falsehoods when the truth is unavailable or not seductive enough." He lifted a shoulder in nonchalance. "I am accustomed to their cowardly tactics."

"Yeah, well, I'm not. And I don't need to be dragged into your mess."

Wariness drew his eyebrows together for an instant, and then all expression was wiped from his face. "What does this have to do with you? Did my brothers speak to you?"

His voice was low and steady and mimicked the same unconcern he obviously wanted her to see. But for a second, she'd seen something else in his eyes. Something resembling fear.

"Speak up," he commanded when she was silently lost in her thoughts.

His rude tone erased any budding sympathy she felt and she glared at him. "Alex told me about the reporters who came poking around. That they want to know about you and your mother."

"What does this have to do with you?"

"For some reason, Alex thought I had seen or heard something yesterday." Memories of Shay's kisses flashed, and she gritted her teeth as heat climbed her face.

Staring back at her, he seemed confused or surprised at first, and then a smug grin curved his mouth. "What did you tell him?"

Resentment pushed away her embarrassment. "You may think this is all fun and games, or some big joke, but I work with these people. I like and respect them, and I care what they think of me. Heck, the Colemans gave me my first real home."

When he frowned with curiosity, she realized she'd blabbed too much. Her history at the orphanage wasn't a secret, but she didn't like to talk about it, either.

Khalid stomped his front hooves as he grew impatient and she was grateful for the distraction. She turned her attention to soothing him and hoped Shay would get the hint and leave.

"Where did you grow up, Olivia?"

She'd planned on ignoring him, until he said her name. His English was only slightly accented—just enough to send pleasant shivers up her spine. When he said her name, he made it sound like some exotic flower blooming in the middle of an oasis.

"Not far from here," she said, shrugging.

"Your family has a ranch?"

She shook her head and busied herself with adjusting Khalid's bridle.

"Ah, a woman of mystery."

The unexpected teasing in his voice made her glance his way. The curve of his lips, the whiteness of his teeth stole her breath. "I grew up in an orphanage."

His smile slid to a puzzled frown.

"It's where a bunch of kids who've been abandoned or whose parents died live together."

"I am familiar with the concept." He studied her face until she looked away. Thankfully she'd seen no pity in his expression. Only curiosity. "Your parents, they are dead?"

"I don't know."

"How old were you when…" He hesitated, a trace of compassion lowering his voice and unnerving her.

"When they abandoned me?" She looked directly at him so he'd see there was no need for pity. "I was a baby. I hadn't even uttered my first word yet. Too bad they didn't stick around to see how great I turned out."

Shay raised his head a little, clearly taken aback by

her attitude. And then a strange smile lifted his lips. "It certainly is a pity they did not. They would have been most pleased. I am truly sorry for their loss."

Livy glared back at him. Was he making fun of her?

He reached out a hand that she tried unsuccessfully to dodge, and he hooked two fingers under her chin and lifted it until their eyes met. "You are an amazing woman. I admire your spirit."

She blinked, surprised by the sincerity in his gaze, the warmth in his touch. Of course, she'd practically yanked the compliment out of him. Sometimes she wished she could just keep her big mouth shut.

She stepped back, breaking contact. "The people at the orphanage were good to me. Father Michael treated us all as if we were his own kids. So don't feel sorry for me."

"Why should I? As I said, it is your parents I pity."

That did it. Livy could take just about anything but blatant kindness. She swallowed hard and turned away. "I don't mean to be rude, but I'm really busy with Khalid."

"Fine. I will enjoy watching you train."

She sighed. "I'd think you'd want to spend time with your mother."

"My mother is in the ground."

Her chest tightened at the harshness in his voice. But he didn't look angry or upset. Surprised, maybe. And then she saw that hint of uncertainty she'd seen earlier.

"I meant Rose," she said, fascinated by the small tic at his clenched jaw.

His expression slowly relaxed, and one side of his mouth lifted. "I see you are seeking my attention again."

Her gaze immediately raised to his. Pure suggestion

darkened the blue of his eyes. She sucked in a breath, wary…excited…scared to death at his total absorption with her mouth.

Slowly exhaling, she struggled to recall the thread of their conversation. Recognition dawned. She snorted. "Nice try."

Shay frowned, his gaze narrowing. "I beg your pardon?"

"You're trying to distract me, because you don't want to talk about anything personal. Tough. I spilled, now it's your turn. What's your problem? If I had a mother like Rose, I'd—I'd be beyond ecstatic."

His look of stunned disbelief was almost comical. "How dare you speak to me this way."

"Really? Why was it okay to give me the third-degree? Now I know why Rose had been so anxious this past week."

"This is none of your concern." He started to walk away.

Livy grabbed his arm. "You don't know, do you?"

He obviously wanted to bolt, but curiosity gleamed in his eyes and he didn't pull away from her. But nor did he ask her what she meant.

"You have no idea how lucky you are." She let her hand drop, half expecting him to leave. He didn't. "Your mother didn't abandon you. You were taken away from her. She loves you. King Zak loves you. Your brothers…everyone wanted you."

He stared at her, saying nothing, until she almost wished he would leave. "You do not understand," he finally said, his voice quiet, subdued.

"Maybe not. But you don't understand what it's like not to belong anywhere. You couldn't. You have the best of both worlds."

"You have a place here, do you not?"

She smiled. "Yup, I do, and I'm grateful for it every minute of every day." Khalid threw his head back and snorted loudly. Livy laughed and stroked his muscled neck. "Yes, I'm grateful for you, too. You are the best Arabian in the entire world. And Prince is the best quarter horse."

She glanced at Shay. He was staring in moody silence, his gaze not focused on anything in particular as far as she could tell. "Earth to Shay, Earth to Shay."

He slowly turned to her, sighing in disgust. "Why do you insist upon calling me that ridiculous name?"

She shrugged, not wanting to point out the name reminded her of that crazy kid from the orphanage. "Because no one else calls you that. And it suits you."

His gaze narrowed. "And if I truly wish to not be called this?"

"I reckon everyone ought to be called what he or she wants. So I'll respect your wishes," she said, sighing, then adjusted Khalid's bit. His growing impatience reminded her that she had a job to do and the sooner she finished, the sooner she could spend time with Prince.

The annual Hill Country Breakneck Race was next week, and she and Prince aimed to win the over fifteen-thousand-dollar grand prize. She had to.

"All right." He waved a hand as if he were suddenly bored with the conversation. "If it pleases you, call me…Shay."

Livy grinned. That was something, coming from him. "And if you want to watch me train Khalid, I don't mind."

The smug curve of his mouth told her he wasn't interested in whether she minded or not. "It will be a pleasure.'' With a quick bow of his head, he left the ring and took a seat on one of the bleachers.

Khalid loved showing off, and Livy had to snap the lead twice to get his attention. It was bad enough that she had to muster all her willpower not to keep glancing over at Shay.

Although she'd never been one to hold a grudge, she especially liked this new side of him. Some folks said the rich were different from everybody else, and she supposed that was true. Shay sure was different. But she also figured that didn't keep him from having problems just like poor folks had. Because in spite of all his bluster, she'd seen the pain and uncertainty in his eyes.

From the risers, Sharif watched Olivia guide the spirited colt in a circle. Like a true champion, Khalid quickly settled down and responded to Olivia's commands as she deftly controlled the pace, rhythm and size of the circle he made. Halfway through the exercise, she had him change direction.

The way she handled the animal was truly art in motion. As soon as she lengthened the rein, Khalid moved forward, stopping and turning as she commanded. It was clear she had a special bond with her charge and the colt seemed eager to please her.

Sharif understood completely.

There was something oddly gratifying in making Olivia smile, in hearing the tinkle of her laughter, seeing the sparks of delight in her violet eyes. She was a unique woman, certainly unlike anyone he had ever met. Olivia certainly had no trouble expressing herself.

A reluctant smile tugged at his mouth. Amazingly he liked it that she spoke her mind. Traditionally, he was of the opinion that most women had little of importance to say. At least that was true in his country.

Or perhaps his demeanor had not invited conversation.

The sudden thought surprised him. It was not a pleasant one. He had far graver concerns than to ponder the oddities of women. Especially a pint-size one, in particular, who made him think about family and gratitude and other things better left alone.

"They're really something, aren't they?"

His head jerked at the sound of Rose's voice. If she wondered what he was doing out here, watching a woman who had poured water over his head, her expression gave nothing away as she slid in beside him.

He returned his attention to Khalid. "He will be a fine stallion some day."

Rose propped her feet up on the bench in front of them and rested her elbows on her knees. A knowing smile lurked at the corners of her mouth, annoying Sharif. He had purposely not mentioned Olivia, and Rose knew it.

"Yes, indeed. Khalid is as fine a horse as his father. Jabbar was just a colt himself when we fled Sorajhee. He's done well here in Texas."

Confused, Sharif turned to look at her. "You said 'we.' You speak of my brothers?"

"That's right. When Alex was almost four and the twins had just turned three we left Sorajhee. Right after your father was murdered." Her smile turned bittersweet and she looked off toward Khalid and Olivia again.

"And you came straight to Texas?"

She frowned at him. "Didn't King Zak tell you the whole story?"

"I am sure he did." Embarrassed, Sharif looked away. "I may not have been paying enough attention."

Her tone held none of the disapproval he expected when she said, "Good. It allows me to personally explain what happened. Do you want to hear it?"

He nodded, then thought better of it. "Unless it will be too painful for you."

She reached out and squeezed his hand, and he experienced an odd warmth. Much like the security he had felt when his mother, Queen Nadirah, had sung him lullabies years ago. "It's always painful to think about how my children were separated from me, but I think it's important that you understand our past."

He swallowed. "I would like to understand." His gaze strayed toward Olivia. Even from this distance, he could see the curiosity in her face.

She had no one who could unfold her past for her, to let her know the circumstances of her abandonment. Although he could not think of a single valid reason for forsaking a child, especially with no explanation. Such an act was despicable and cowardly to his thinking, no matter the reason.

But he also believed knowledge, regardless of how difficult it was to take, was easier than the emotionally crippling claws of uncertainty.

Rose respected his meditative silence and continued to watch Olivia and Khalid, but when he turned to her, she took her cue. "Your father was in favor of the unification of Sorajhee and your country, Balahar. Some opposed this idea, his brother, your uncle Azzam included. It was during a protest demonstration that your father was murdered.

"I was insane with grief, and when I thought all the evidence pointed to Azzam as the person responsible,

I immediately fled to England with your three brothers. If Azzam was crazy enough to have his own brother murdered, I couldn't be sure he wouldn't harm your brothers, since they were heirs to the throne.''

She paused to watch Olivia try to persuade Khalid to adopt a flattering show stance, one that would allow him to be judged favorably.

Sharif wasn't fooled. Her interest in the training had more to do with taking an emotional break. Was this therapeutic or too painful for her? Perhaps he should not have asked her to revisit the past. The truth was, he already knew most of the story, but somehow, hearing it come from her was comforting.

Rose slowly shook her head. "It's really amazing to think Khalid is Jabbar's offspring. Jabbar was just this gangly, fuzzy little creature when we smuggled him out of Sorajhee. But even then we knew he would be a good foundation stallion, something for the boys to take with them, and know he was part of their heritage.''

She looked apologetically at Sharif and smiled. "I've digressed. Old age does that to you.''

"You are not old.'' He did not know who was more surprised over his impulsive, defensive remark—himself or Rose. He shrugged a shoulder. "You are still very beautiful.''

"Thank you, Sharif.'' Her cheeks flushed a soft pink that made her look even younger. "You remind me of your father.''

He stiffened slightly. "After England, you came here to Texas?''

"No. I said goodbye to the boys in England and I returned home to search out the truth behind your father's death. I knew they would be safe with Randy, who would take them back to Boston where he lived, and I had no idea what I'd be facing back in Sorajhee.''

"Why did you return? Why did you not go to America?''

"Alex was heir to the throne even though he was only four years old, and next in line were the twins. I wasn't convinced they'd be safe until the murderer was caught. Besides, grief does strange things to a person.''

"That was the last time you saw them?''

She pressed her lips together, stared out past Olivia and Khalid, and nodded. "My suspicion that your uncle Azzam was behind the assassination was confirmed by his wife Layla. Now I know she was the one responsible, and that she'd been feeding me wrong information. But I'm not sure we'll ever know the whole truth.'' She slid him a reluctant look, her eyes filled with pain. "I did something really horrible.''

Sharif quickly covered her hand with his, startling her into silence. "I know what happened. I would have done the same in your place.''

"But it looks as though Azzam was innocent, and I tried to take his life.''

Their gazes locked and, by tacit agreement, they allowed a comfortable silence to blanket them. Sharif did not need to hear the rest. He knew Layla had manipulated Azzam into having Rose committed to a sanitarium in Paris, while she continued to pretend to be Rose's friend. Layla had even sent word to Randy claiming Rose was dead, and convinced him that faking the boys' deaths would keep them safe, and therefore, allowing Azzam to seize the throne. He figured that was when Randy Coleman had decided to move them all to Texas.

What Sharif did want to know was why, after his

birth, Rose had let him go. Intellectually he understood she could not have raised him in a sanitarium, but the irrational child inside him could not accept it.

"What are you thinking, Sharif?"

He shook his head and stared out at Olivia. Her hat had slipped off and hung down her back, leaving her hair a tousled mess of light brown waves with a few comical spikes. She clearly did not give the matter a thought. Her attention was focused entirely on Khalid.

The more he learned of her, the more remarkable she seemed. Although her childhood may not have been pleasant, for her, it was over. It was that simple.

"Sharif?"

He snapped out of his preoccupied silence. "Khalid will bring a fine price. I must speak to your brother about what he is looking for."

Disappointment strained her features as she briefly studied his face, as though she were searching for emotions he was not willing to communicate. Finally she said, "Oh, I doubt that little rascal is for sale."

"Everything has a price."

Her expression was bittersweet. "Not everything. Do you want to walk me back to the house? I'll make us some tea."

Sharif thought for a moment. He noted with amazement that he was tempted to follow her back. Even more amazing, he had the overwhelming urge to talk with Olivia again. "I want to watch them train a while longer."

"Certainly." She stood and smiled, but he could tell she was disappointed.

"Rose?"

She had started to leave, but she stopped and turned expectantly.

"I should like some tea later, if you are free."

"Of course." Her lips curved in such a grateful smile, it made him feel both happy and ashamed. "I have nothing planned this afternoon. Actually, I was hoping I could spend as much time with you as possible."

His shame vanished, and his defenses started to rise.

"I'm not pushing," she said quickly, obviously having interpreted his thoughts. "I just wanted to let you know I'm free to do whatever you'd like."

"I understand. I should be returning to the house before long."

This time her smile was so tentative it made him uncomfortable. Yet why should he be responsible for her happiness? She had three other sons.

He purposely averted his face as she walked away. After he knew she had covered a good distance, he glanced toward her retreating form. But his attention was diverted by his approaching servant.

Recognizing the urgency in Omar's stride, Sharif squinted at the roll his servant carried. As he got closer, Sharif realized it was a newspaper.

Omar said nothing as he opened it in front of Sharif.

Words were not necessary.

Across the front page was a large photo of him and Olivia. One that left no room for interpretation.

Chapter Six

A string of curses, both in his own tongue and then in English, flew through his head. Outwardly he straightened and dismissed Omar with a wave of his hand. The man had become a friend to him over the years and Sharif had probably just wounded him.

But he could not keep his thoughts clear.

He stared down at the image of him bare chested, and Olivia's shirt slipping down her shoulder, exposing her skin. She looked a little dazed, her eyes wide and her mouth slightly parted, and anyone with any sense would know they had just kissed. Or more.

Of course people would choose to think more had happened. All they needed was one tantalizing picture such as this, he thought, as his gaze scanned the accompanying article.

"Hey, Shay, did you see what Khalid just did?"

At the sound of Olivia's voice, he quickly rerolled the paper and looked up. She was leading the colt toward the risers, a big grin on her face.

The closer she got, the more her smile faded. She stopped a few feet in front of him, frowning. "What's wrong? You look like someone beat you to your place at the lunch table."

"Have you finished here?"

"I've finished with Khalid for today." Her gaze lowered to the rolled newspaper. "But I have to work with Prince for a while. Why?"

Sharif said nothing. He rubbed the side of his neck and stared off toward the lake that pooled at the bottom of the slope. Only a slice of it could be seen through the trees, but he fixed his attention on the calming blue water.

He owed Olivia no explanation. He was just as much a victim. In fact, in his position, he had more with which to be concerned. He was royalty. She was a servant.

Khalid snorted and stepped high with impatience.

"Walk with me," Olivia said, and headed toward the stable. "Maybe the exercise will wipe that lemon-sucking look off your face."

He shook his head as he fell into step beside her. She had a strange way with words. He wondered what combinations she would devise when she saw the photograph.

"Well, let's see. I haven't been near you for the past forty-five minutes, so I couldn't have done anything to get you steamed." An impish smile tugged at her mouth, and she looked at him with those big innocent violet eyes. "You think I'm gonna ask you about your conversation with Rose, don't you? That's why you're giving me the silent treatment."

She laughed. "I hate to break it to you, but if I get an itch to know something, nothing short of a flash flood is going to slow me down."

They got to the stable, and she started to carefully remove Khalid's exercise bandages from his front legs. She was too preoccupied with her task to notice that

Sharif had not responded. In truth, he still did not know if or what he would tell her. Perhaps she would not even see the newspaper. Possibly she would not be concerned. Most women he knew would be content to be linked with him.

Besides, he had his own problems stemming from this piece of pseudo garbage journalism with which to deal. King Zak would be furious. With the recent discovery of Rose and the revelation of Sharif's true heritage, there had already been enough fodder for international headlines.

And now, King Zak's adopted son, the heir to Balahar, was cavorting with a commoner.

"Hold this, would you?" Olivia handed him the bandages she had already removed.

As soon as their fingers touched, Sharif's blood ignited. It was almost a physical blow, the sensation was so strong. Part of it was her eyes and the way she looked at him, the way her tongue darted out to moisten her lower lip.

He honestly had not thought too much about their kiss, but right now, all he could think about was pressing his mouth to hers again. Instead he cleared his throat.

She blinked and withdrew her hand to start on Khalid's back legs. "Now, if your holding those bandages violates some royal law about doing too much manual labor, then you go right ahead and drop them."

She was teasing him, of course, but her voice sounded funny, and maybe a little hoarse. He wondered what she would do if he did kiss her again. If he palmed her breasts and entered her mouth with his tongue.

"Well, if that don't beat all!" A male voice filtered

down the hall along with a chorus of chuckles. "Who would've thunk it?"

"Now, don't go jumpin' to no conclusions," another man said, this time closer.

Olivia's eyes met Sharif's, a flicker of panic in them, and she grabbed his shirt and pulled him into the stall beside her. Then she raised a silencing finger to her lips. He nodded, torn between being in agreement and feeling insulted.

"What do you mean? I don't have to jump to no conclusions. Everything is concluded for me right here in black and white."

It was agony standing this close to her. Even after being out in the warm sun with Khalid, she smelled good. Her womanly scent filled his nostrils, and her hip pressed against him in a perfect spot. He moved his chin, and it brushed the top of her hair.

"I don't give a pig's ass about that picture. Ain't you ever heard about how those tabloid people use computers to change stuff? Make couples look like they're in the same room when they ain't."

"This isn't a tabloid, you numskull. This here is a genuine, respectable newspaper," the other man said, and Sharif clenched his teeth, comprehension dawning. "Besides, Livy isn't anybody famous. Why would they use her?"

She stiffened and tilted her head back to look up at him. Confusion and fear darkened her eyes.

Should he speak up and end the men's conversation, or remain silent and hope they quickly passed out of earshot? Decisiveness had always been Sharif's strong suit. Now his thoughts froze.

"Thing is, she really surprised the hell out of me." The voice was already growing fainter as the men appeared to be headed outside. "Here I thought she was all innocent and pure. Sure had me fooled."

The second man responded, but they were already too far away to hear what he'd said.

Olivia's mouth dropped open, but other than that, she seemed paralyzed. When she looked at him again, her eyes had grown suspiciously glassy.

His chest tightened. Her anger he could take, but not this wounded look. He ran his hand up her arm, then cupped her shoulder. "Olivia, I—"

Her gaze flew to the rolled newspaper. "Let me see it."

"Maybe it is best if—"

She jerked away from him. "Give me the damn paper."

He had no choice. From the look on her enraged face, she would either start crying or screaming at any moment. He handed her the newspaper.

She tore it open, and then stared at the picture for a long time. First shock, then disbelief, drained the color from her face. She started shaking her head, her attention absorbed by their compromising images. "How did someone take this picture?"

"That flash yesterday, I knew it was from a camera... I tried to catch him."

She lifted her gaze. "You knew about this?"

"That is why I left the stables so abruptly yesterday."

"You knew about this?" she repeated, her accusing eyes brimming with anger and resentment.

He straightened, moving a fraction away from her. "I did not know the photograph would be published. No."

"What the hell did you think they were going to do with it? Gift wrap it and send it to us?"

He ignored her sarcasm, even though his temper had also been ignited. She had no right to attack him. He was as much a victim. More, in fact. He was a public figure. News of this fictitious tryst implied by the photograph was bound to reach Balahar and fuel the whispers about him. Their future king of not-so-royal stock was now bedding commoners.

The thought stuck in his throat like a hard lump of bread that would not go down.

"You had no right to keep this from me." Olivia stepped back and slumped against the stable wall. Her voice was small, accented by defeat. "You should have told me yesterday."

Every muscle in his body went as taut as harp strings. He would not accept the responsibility or the blame. He grabbed the newspaper from her hand and purposefully looked at the picture, and then at her. "You do not look as though you are objecting here."

She let out what sounded like part laugh, part sob. "You don't get it, do you? Were you even listening to me earlier?"

Silently Sharif lifted his chin.

"You're used to reporters following you around. So your face is splashed across a television screen, or under the headlines of a newspaper. I'm sure this isn't your first *scandal*. But this is my home. This is where I wake up every day. It's the first place I really felt I belonged. These guys are my friends. Or were." She briefly closed her eyes and pain washed over her face. "But now—"

Shaking her head, she pushed off the wall and struggled to straighten, as if the effort was more than she could handle. When she lumbered past him, she did not even give him a second's glance.

The helplessness that swirled around Sharif was unfamiliar, and anger boiled in his belly. "Where are you going?"

She did not respond, only stopped to murmur something to Khalid, then continued out of the stables with wooden steps and a heavy slump to her shoulders.

In her wake, the silence was maddening. The powerlessness threatened to drown him. The anger, he welcomed. When he flung the newspaper against the wall, the thud it made was hardly satisfying.

He could not worry about her. His father would be furious. Sharif had to get to him before anyone else did, explain the photograph suggested a falsehood.

His thoughts unexpectedly flickered to Rose. She, too, would be disappointed in him.

He picked up the paper and flung it against the wall again. Why was he concerning himself with the American woman's opinion of him? He took a deep breath.

He knew why. And he did not like it. Queen Nadirah, the true mother of his heart, deserved his loyalty.

Khalid snorted, demanding attention. Sharif picked up the paper, rolled it up and stuck it under his arm before he went to the colt. He mentally shook his head when he finally realized Khalid was reacting to his childish display of flinging the paper. Horses were sensitive to sound, he knew, and the thuds as well as a few choice curses had alarmed the animal.

As soon as Sharif reached in to stroke the colt's neck, his ears went forward and Sharif knew he was forgiven. Or maybe Khalid was just curious, wondering who this strange man was who was upsetting his trainer.

Horses were wonderful creatures. Intelligent, highly sensitive and very expressive. Most people underestimated them. Not Sharif. And certainly not Olivia. When she worked with Khalid, they were a true team, almost a single unit, their bond appeared so great. In a way, she was his adopted mother.

His thoughts immediately returned to Rose. And the bond that they, too, shared. But it was all too much for him to ponder right now. He had explanations to deliver. He gave Khalid a final pat and headed out of the stables.

After the subdued lighting inside, the sun seemed brighter and more obtrusive. Olivia was nowhere in sight. Not that he expected her to stay visible. But he did wish to speak to her again after she had calmed down and realized the situation was not so tragic. Or reversible.

At least he could assure her she had no need to fear further incident. As Sharif's American college friend used to say, it was time that Sharif kept his nose clean. If not for his own sake, for that of his father's.

As he rounded the corner, he caught sight of the sprawling beige-colored main house off to the left and realized that, lost in thought, he had veered off course. A smaller house, probably the hands' bunkhouse, was nearby to his right.

Had he unconsciously followed Olivia? He imagined she was locked away in her room by now, waiting for the shock and pain to subside. He thrust a hand through his hair and revised his course. Now was not the time to talk to her.

He had only made it a couple of feet when he heard the male laughter. It came from the side of the bunkhouse. He slowed his pace and again altered his course when he thought he heard Olivia's name.

"You seen that paper yet? The one with the picture of Livy and that sheikh dude?"

"What are you talking about, Corky? She doesn't rub elbows with those kind of people."

Sharif immediately recognized the first man's voice, and stopped in his tracks, every fiber of his being tensed with rage and disgust.

The first man laughed. "It wasn't his elbow she was rubbing, I tell ya. Wish I'd had me a roll in the hay with her a time or two. Maybe it's not too late."

"Livy? You been hitting the bottle again?"

It's the first place I really felt I belonged.

Olivia's plaintive voice echoed in his head, and the sickness came in several waves. He had been so bloody self-absorbed. What had he done to her?

"Okay, how much you wanna bet? A hundred bucks says the picture I show you has you eating crow."

"You're crazy, and I don't wanna hear any more about Livy."

The second man's voice had lost conviction, and Sharif called in every measure of self-control at his command.

"Fine. That'll leave her free and clear for me to take a poke at her."

Reason and sanity completely deserted him. He strode around the corner, too incensed to relish the stunned look on the two cowboys' faces.

The shorter blond one started mumbling something, enough that Sharif recognized his vile voice as the instigator and headed straight for him. The man backed up, and Sharif stopped at arm's length in front of him.

''Do you have something to say about Olivia?'' he asked with a deceptive half smile.

The two men exchanged sheepish looks. ''I dunno,'' the shorter one said. ''No, I don't suppose I have nothing to say.'' He briskly shook his head. ''Nothing at all.''

''Good. Then keep your mouth shut,'' he said calmly. Then punched the man in the middle of his bulbous red nose.

This time when the flashes went off, Sharif was too damn mad to care.

LIVY STARED at the big mess on her bed. All the clothes she owned lay scattered across the quilt or hung from the lone chair in her room. Not that there was all that much to pack, but she was about as organized as a heap of pickup sticks.

What was she doing, anyway? She couldn't just run out on the Colemans. They might be disappointed in her, maybe even madder than a bee with no honey, but they couldn't afford to be short one hand. Besides, where would she and Prince go?

And then there was Khalid. God, she'd miss him.

She sank to the edge of the bed and sighed. She was going to have to do it. Walk up to the main house and apologize on her knees. Vi had been in such a weird state lately, Livy cringed at the thought of facing her. Not that Vi had ever said an unkind word to her, but her recent moodiness had everyone walking on eggshells already. Livy figured it was some female problem she had to look forward to when she got to be that age.

And of course there was Rose. Livy threw herself backward and fell heavily into the mattress.

Damn that Shay.

She sniffed and stared out her tiny window. Part of her knew it wasn't his fault, but she still thought he should have warned her. It was going to be especially hard facing Mickey. Next to Jessica Coleman, he was her closest friend.

Although he had tried to defend her, bless him, by refusing to believe the picture was real, in the long run, a photo would be darn hard to argue against.

In a perverse way, she wished she had a copy of it. She'd been so stunned earlier, she hadn't gotten a good enough look at it. Probably just as well. If she never saw Shay's face again, it would suit her fine.

Because what made her feel crummiest of all was his obvious indifference. He didn't give a hoot about her. All he'd thought about was his own reputation, as if it didn't have a few black marks on it already. He was probably a girl-in-every-tent kind of guy. If only they hadn't gotten along so well earlier. She had actually started to like him.

The knock on the door startled her and she bolted upright, then dabbed at her cheeks, just in case. For a second she let her hand hover at the doorknob and thought about pretending she wasn't there, but facing people had to be done sooner or later.

She cleared her throat, swallowed hard, then opened the door with a sad lack of enthusiasm. "Rose?"

"Hi." The older woman's gentle smile said it all.

Of course she knew. For Livy to think otherwise would be pure fantasy. "Hi," she returned lamely.

"Mind if I come in?"

Livy shrugged sheepishly as she stepped aside. "The place is a mess."

"Ah, spring cleaning, I see," Rose said, ignoring the battered suitcase lying open at the foot of the bed.

"Yeah. Sort of." Livy scurried to clear her only chair of the red flannel underwear strewn over it.

"Thank you." Rose sat down, still managing to look regal in a pair of jeans and a plain blue blouse.

"I know why you're here," Livy blurted. "And I can't tell you how sorry I am."

Rose frowned. "I think you've mistaken the reason for my visit, because it's certainly nothing for you to apologize for."

Livy sank back down on the edge of the bed. Could her mouth be any bigger? At Rose's laughter, she blinked.

"I think we are talking about the same thing, except you're making too much of it."

Livy choked. "Now I know we're not on the same wavelength."

"The newspaper picture?"

Fresh embarrassment rolled in her stomach and erupted into her cheeks. The temperature seemed to have soared a good twenty degrees.

Rose leaned forward to take Livy's hand. "I'm not saying it isn't a big deal, or you shouldn't have any reaction. Being made a public figure can be daunting and sometimes humiliating." She gave Livy's hand a reassuring squeeze. "And, yes, I'd bet you're very embarrassed about now. But you've done nothing for which you should be ashamed. Or sorry."

Livy stared silently at her. The older woman had the same kind eyes she always had, but this was a joke, right?

"Ever heard the saying 'this too shall pass'?"

Livy shook her head.

Rose squeezed her hand one more time before releasing it and leaning back in her chair. "It means today's news will be history by tomorrow. It means in time you'll forget this ever happened."

"Wish I could slip into a coma until then."

Rose laughed softly. "Been there, done that, as they say. It's not fun."

Livy suddenly remembered she'd heard rumors about Rose being drugged and kept locked away in a sanitarium for years. Clamping a hand over her big mouth, she mumbled, "I'm so sorry."

"Stop saying that. I'm here, alive and well, aren't I? Proof that the human spirit has amazing resilience." Her smile widened. "That was a message for you, in case you missed it."

Livy smiled, too. How could she not? She truly wished she'd had a mother like Rose. "Does everybody know?"

"Just about." Her expression was sympathetic. "King Zak is having a talk with Sharif right now."

Livy scrubbed at her face. "Oh, boy, he's got to be steaming."

"With Sharif, not with you. But it'll be okay. I had a word or two with him."

"Why aren't you upset?"

The outside corners of Rose's eyes crinkled with amusement. "Why should I be? I'm pleased my son has such excellent taste."

Taken aback, she wasn't sure if she correctly grasped Rose's meaning. "I'm not sure I, um…" She shrugged helplessly.

"Sharif is good-looking and charming just like his father, Ibrahim. And for that matter, King Zak." A faint pink seeped into Rose's complexion. "He's my son and I love him dearly. But if that ego of his gets any bigger, King Zak will have to buy a larger jet to get them home.''

Livy coughed.

Rose sighed. ''I suppose he isn't any different from other young men his age who have the world at their feet. But I was honestly beginning to worry.''

''He isn't *that* bad. Just a little arrogant, maybe.'' Livy couldn't believe she had just said that to Shay's own mother. But the older woman had a way of putting her at total ease.

''And self-absorbed,'' Rose added.

''He's been through a lot, too. It had to be hard to find out he was adopted after all those years.''

''You're a very wise woman, Olivia Smith. But even wise women make foolish mistakes sometimes.''

Livy stiffened. ''I don't have any fantasies about Shay, if that's what you mean. That picture was very misleading. I understand there is nothing between us.''

A mysterious smile curved Rose's lips as she stood to leave. ''That's not what I meant at all.''

Chapter Seven

Something was wrong. Sharif studied his father's subdued face. He was not nearly as angry as Sharif had expected him to be. In fact, he had said little, only listened to Sharif's explanation with a noncommittal expression. It was almost eerie.

Before she had left, Rose, too, had been surprisingly reserved. Not even one brow lifted in disapproval, and her eyes remained kind and almost sympathetic. Her only question had pertained to Olivia's welfare.

"You have told me everything?" his father asked after a long silence had stretched.

"I swear it on my mother's grave," Sharif said, and received his first look of displeasure.

"Be careful, my son."

That was all his father had said. All he needed to say. Because, oddly, as soon as the words were out of Sharif's mouth, he regretted them. True, Queen Nadirah was already in the ground. However, Rose was not.

"How do you plan to handle this?" his father asked, a thoughtful frown lining his face.

"I could ignore the insinuation. It will, of course, fade away in the face of more worthy news." Sharif's gaze strayed out the window. The bunkhouse was not visible from where he sat in the living room, but he could picture Olivia there, huddled in her room, afraid to face her peers. "Or I could call a reputable reporter from the paper and grant him an exclusive interview in exchange for some sort of retraction."

"You cannot retract what has been captured on film."

"True, but I can give an explanation, prove that nothing happened."

"Can you?"

Sharif grunted as he met his father's eyes. "That depends on how much I want to humble myself."

King Zak's left brow lifted with interest. "Why would you do this? You never grant interviews. Much less concede to humility."

He half smiled at the dig and looked away again. "Times and things change. You said so yourself."

"Is it the girl?"

Sharif honestly did not know. So many confusing thoughts had been swirling inside his head. "Not in the way you are thinking."

His father laughed. "You want to explain my thoughts to me?"

He frowned at the lightness of the conversation, at his father's high spirits. He had expected him to be furious. "She is not accustomed to the media. Nor is she the kind of woman who would be, shall we say, found in the sort of position the newspaper implied."

"And you are concerned for her reputation?"

Uncomfortable suddenly, he shrugged a shoulder. "Yes, of course."

His father's mouth curved in a satisfied smile. "Maybe that dousing of water she gave you did some good."

It was not like the king to jest. He was normally more reserved, but he seemed more relaxed in the past couple of days than Sharif had ever seen him. That made Sharif wonder how much Rose's presence had to do with it.

"She is very spirited," Sharif finally said. "Has no trouble speaking her mind. And stubborn? I doubt there is a camel on this earth more headstrong than that woman."

"Really?"

Mirth formed the single word, and Sharif glared at his father, who did nothing to hide his amusement. "So why would I have an affair with a woman such as this? It happened as I told you. I lost my footing when the horse nudged me and I had to remove my muddy shirt."

King Zak gave him a conciliatory nod, but amusement still gleamed in his eyes. "Perhaps you should have a talk with the woman and decide together how this should be handled."

"Her name is Olivia." Sharif mumbled an expletive when his father chuckled. He stood, anxious to be alone. "Perhaps I will go talk to her."

"Sharif?"

He had already turned to leave, but at the serious tone in his father's voice, he stopped.

"Make sure that is all you do with Olivia."

"COME ON, SMITH, either get your lazy butt out here and muck out the stalls or knock my dang hat off."

Livy still hadn't given in to a good cry over the events of yesterday, but hearing Mickey's familiar voice just about did her in. He'd defended her yesterday, refused to believe that the picture was real. She'd be forever grateful, but for now, she snuggled deeper under her quilt and pressed her lips together.

"Look, if I have to go in there and drag you out, I'll do it. You know I will," Mickey said, and she pictured him getting all red in the face like he did when he got mad or excited or embarrassed.

She couldn't help but grin. "Yeah? You and which army?"

Even through the door, she heard his sigh of relief. "I don't need no help with a little squirt like you."

Flinging off the quilt, she swung her legs out of bed and padded to the door in stockinged feet. She was already dressed in jeans and a light blue denim shirt because earlier she'd made two unsuccessful attempts to leave her room.

And then yesterday's conversation between Mickey and the new hand, Corky Higgins, replayed in her head and she'd dived back under the covers. She knew she had to face them all sooner or later, but later sounded just fine.

When she opened the door, Mickey nearly toppled over her. "You don't even have enough sense to not lean on a door that's about to open and you think you're gonna get the best of me. Yeah, right."

He grinned. "Glad your face ain't all puffy and your eyes red, or I wouldn't know what the heck to do."

"Well, that was subtle and tactful."

"If you say so. I don't even know what that means." His grin widened. "I see you're dressed to do some mucking."

She grabbed him by the shirt, yanked him inside and closed the door. "What's everybody saying?"

Obviously startled, he stumbled over the candy bar

wrappings littering the floor and sank into the chair. "About what?"

"Don't, Mickey."

He gave a sheepish shrug. "Us old-timers don't believe a word of that article. And as far as that picture—" he shrugged again "—it don't mean nothing."

"What are the rest of the guys saying?"

"They're idiots."

"Mickey."

"Ah, come on, Livy, what do you think they're saying? Especially after that dude—" He stopped himself and met her gaze with wary eyes. Then he looked away. "Those guys are just jealous."

She didn't even smile at his left-handed compliment. "What dude?"

"Ah, Liv, are you gonna ask me what I had for breakfast, too?"

"Shay?" At his puzzled frown, she added, "The guy in the picture with me."

Mickey abruptly stood. "I know you didn't do nothing with him, and most of the other fellas do, too," he said, on his way to the door. "You wanna find anything else out? Then get your butt out here and muck the stalls."

"Mickey?"

He stopped, the doorknob in his hand, and sighed. "Yeah?"

When he turned to look at her, she knocked off his hat.

LIVY SKIPPED LUNCH because she still couldn't bring herself to sit across the table from Corky Higgins, or the rest of the guys, for that matter. Besides, all the chocolate she ate wasn't sitting too well in her stomach, and after mucking out twenty stalls, food was the last thing on her mind.

Mickey had been sweet enough to offer to help her, even though she'd cheated when she knocked his hat off by blindsiding him. But she'd actually been glad for the chore. It kept her out of sight. She just wished she could rein in her wild thoughts.

Should she go and talk to the Colemans? Assume Rose had spoken on her behalf? Pretend nothing happened? Which was actually the truth. Other than a little kissing. The reminder brought goose bumps to the surface of her skin.

Damn that Shay.

The only thing she was sure of was that she was staying clear of *him*.

Boundless energy and a need to keep busy had her finished with her work earlier than usual, even with the late start. She picked up her grooming kit and headed for Prince's stall. He'd make her feel better. There'd be no judgment in his eyes. And a big plus—they'd be alone.

Prince wasn't in a good mood, which was unusual for him. As soon as he saw her, his ears went back and he turned around and presented her with his rump.

"Well, thanks, and here I was coming by for moral support, you big turkey." Sighing, Livy put down the kit. She was being too sensitive. Prince didn't always like being groomed, and he'd probably seen the dandy brush sticking out of the bucket.

"I knew you would come here today."

At the sound of Shay's low voice, she jumped, then spun around.

"No wonder Prince would rather face the wall. I don't blame him." Her heart raced at the sight of him in worn jeans and a chambray shirt. "What are you doing here?"

"I came to talk to you."

"Too late." She bent to pick up the dandy brush and noticed her hands were shaking. "You should've done your talking before I saw the picture."

"You are right, of course."

Surprised at his admission, she gave him a sideways glance. "Darn straight I'm right." She lifted her chin, and unlatched the stall door. "You're in my way."

He wasn't, really, but he quietly stepped aside, anyway.

"Come on, champ, you're gonna get brushed whether you like it or not. Don't you want to go outside?" She slid into the stall beside Prince and slipped on his lead. She turned around and met Shay's eyes. "Are you still here?"

"Say you will have dinner with me and I will go."

Livy coughed and sputtered. "Prince, did you kick this guy in the head, or something?"

Prince threw his head back and snorted.

"I see your point." She started to stroke the side of his neck but decided her hand would shake again. "It's not safe getting that close to him."

"Well, she did not say no. That is something, huh?"

She jerked around to see who Shay was talking to, but his gaze was directed at Prince, who seemed to agree by bringing his head up and down.

Placing a hand on her hip, she glared at the gelding. "Okay, you traitor, since you seem to be on speaking terms with him, tell him the answer is a definite no."

Prince didn't make a sound. He just looked back with sad, dull eyes.

"He clearly thinks you should have dinner with

me,'' Shay said, with a smile that reached his eyes and made her pulse go berserk.

''And provide another photo op? I don't think so.'' She led Prince out of the stall, wondering if it was wise to go out into the open. From where she usually groomed him, anyone from the side of the main house or the outdoor ring could see her with Shay if he followed her.

And he did.

She sighed with disgust when he carried out her grooming kit. ''Look, I'm sure you already figured out I'm not your type, so what in the heck are you doing?''

''Trying to form a response to the press. So it will please you to know the dinner will be strictly business.''

''Oh.'' The obvious shouldn't have hurt, but it did. He had no real interest in her. ''So, why waste a good meal over discussing something that icky?''

His left eyebrow went up. ''I assume you mean distasteful?''

She stifled a growl. And the juvenile urge to mimic him. ''Whatever.'' Well, that was mature. She reached into the grooming kit with a vengeance. Prince backed up a step.

''Shall I come by for you around seven?''

''No, you can keep your butt in the main house, because I'm not sharing so much as a potato chip with you.''

Anger ignited in his eyes. ''You are refusing me?''

''Hard to believe, isn't it?''

He moved toward her until she was sandwiched between him and Prince. ''Actually, I do not believe it.''

Her breath caught when his fanned her heated cheek.

"That's because your ego doesn't leave enough room for any common sense."

He stared down at her for a long time without speaking. A wave of heat threatened her balance. She knew she should look away; it was dangerous to be held captive by the desire in his dilated eyes. But she couldn't do it. She could barely breathe.

"I have apologized, Olivia," he finally said. "What more do you want from me?"

She swallowed and stepped back so he wouldn't smell her fear. Strange things were happening to her body and her head. Prickly feelings and sappy longings she didn't understand were throwing her off balance.

"Simple," she said in a flip tone. "Leave me alone."

THE SUN WAS CLOSE to setting, and Livy paused outside the stable to admire the streaks of salmon-colored clouds running riot over the lake. Prince was already tucked away in his stall, and all she had to do was put away the grooming kit before she hit the shower.

Normally she loved this time of day when everything looked so still and peaceful, and the twilight hid any flaws. Not that she thought Mother Nature was responsible for any goofs. But man was, at least some of the ranchers who cared more about turning a profit than they did for the land.

The Colemans weren't like that at all. They had a healthy respect for everything green and living. They were good people, and she prayed she hadn't disappointed them.

On the off chance she hadn't, she hoped there wouldn't be another opportunity to do so.

She had to stay as far away from Shay as possible.

Even the fact that she was still annoyed with him for withholding the newspaper from her didn't stop her heart from speeding, or from developing an embarrassing dampness in her south pasture.

And if thinking about the newspaper wasn't enough to cool her engines, all she had to do was remind herself that for him, she was only a plaything, a way to pass the time while he was in Texas. Probably even a way to avoid Rose.

The new thought depressed her. Not just because it was pretty obvious she was way down on Shay's totem pole, but because Rose was a good person, and Livy didn't want to be involved in his avoidance of her in any way.

She sadly shook her head and turned away from the sunset. It was starting to lack luster. The best thing she could do was stay in her tiny area of the world, away from Shay, and hope time sped by.

"I have been looking all over for you!"

Livy turned excitedly at the sound of her friend's voice. "Jessica! When did you get back from Dallas?"

"Just this morning. Man, have I missed out on a bunch of stuff, or what?"

Livy grimaced. "You've already heard? Jeez Louise."

Jessica frowned. "Heard what?"

"I don't know." Livy mentally kicked herself. Maybe her friend wasn't talking about Shay or the newspaper photo. "Tell me what you heard, and I'll tell you if there's anything else."

Jess narrowed her gaze in suspicion and planted both hands on her hips. "All right, spill."

"What?"

"I know you better that that, Livy Smith. Besides, your face is redder than Mama's prize roses."

The Colemans' daughter was only a year older than Livy, and despite their social differences, they had gotten along famously from the first day Livy arrived on the ranch. It helped that they had the same temperament. Although personally, Livy thought Jess was a little more of a wildcat than she was.

"You know the silent treatment isn't going to work with me," Jessica said when Livy had stalled too long. "Better not irritate me. I've got something Rose said you'd be interested in." She patted her jeans back pocket.

"That's low. Really low."

Jess chuckled. "You're way too nosy to hold out, so you might as well give me the dirt."

Livy sighed. It was really better that Jess heard about the Shay fiasco from her. "Have you met your parents' houseguests?"

"I've met King Zak briefly, but I haven't met the boys' brother, Sharif, yet. Have you?"

"Uh, you could say that."

Jessica's eyes sparkled with mischief. "I'm listening."

A thought struck Livy and she cringed. Jessica was a born matchmaker. She'd been hell-bent on bringing Alex and Hannah together, and then Mac and Abbie. Livy had thought it was funny at the time. She didn't now. "And that's all you're doing."

She widened her eyes in innocence. The fact that one was blue and the other green gave her an impish look at the best of times, so her act didn't work.

"Are you teasing me? Do you already know?" Livy asked.

"Know what?"

Her frustrated shriek convinced Livy. "Shay and I got caught by a reporter in, um, well, a strange situation, and it sort of made it to the front page of the paper."

"Sort of?"

Livy shrugged a shoulder and slowly headed for the bunkhouse. She was starting a doozy of a headache.

"Wait a minute." Jess scurried alongside her. "Shay is the boys' brother, Sharif, I take it."

She nodded. "Now, some of the guys around here have the wrong idea."

"Wow! No kidding. Bet you set them straight." She stared at Livy, who remained silent and embarrassed. "Didn't you?"

"Let's just say I'm keeping a low profile."

"But that doesn't sound like—" Jessica stopped in her tracks. "Gosh darn it. You got me all sidetracked, and I almost forgot why I was looking for you. Mac and Abbie had their baby!"

"When?" Livy forgot about Shay and the reporter and everything else, and warm, fuzzy pleasure enfolded her.

"This morning. Her name is Sarah Rose Coleman–El Jeved, and she weighs seven pounds three ounces."

"Jeez, she's gonna be twenty before she can remember her name." Livy laughed along with Jess, but she was so pleased they'd named the little girl after Rose she could burst.

They arrived at the bunkhouse and Jess turned to her with a grin. "So, I guess your low profile is going to have to wait."

Livy frowned back.

"You know how we Colemans love to celebrate.

Barbecue and beer for everyone.'' She glanced at her wristwatch, then started backing away in the direction of the main house. ''It starts in half an hour. Just enough time for you to grab a shower, then pick out your prettiest sundress.''

''My—?'' Livy gasped. ''Don't even think about it.''

Jess stopped and stuck her hand in her back pocket. ''Oops, I almost forgot. Here.''

Livy took the folded paper she handed her. ''I mean it, Jess.''

The other woman only grinned and wiggled her fingers. ''See ya at the party.'' Then she turned and raced toward the house.

Livy stood watching her go and thinking a slew of unladylike words. No way could she show up at the barbecue. It wasn't as if Mac and Abbie and the baby would be there. Probably only Mac, and even so, no one would miss her, anyway.

Jessica would. So would Rose, and she didn't put it past either of them to drag her kicking and screaming to the festivities.

Oh, heck, she'd go for a little while, just long enough to make sure she was seen. But not long enough to get anywhere near His Royal Pain. Exchanging two words with him would probably start tongues wagging. And then, of course, there was all that chemistry zinging between them.

She'd read about that once in one of Jessica's magazines. Livy hadn't believed a word of it. Until she'd met Shay. Damn his hide.

She made it to her room without having to talk to anyone, and stared into her closet. She had only one sundress to her name, and she absolutely wasn't going to wear it. Besides the air being too chilly in the evenings, she didn't want anyone getting the wrong idea. Least of all Shay.

Finally she pulled out a pair of fresh jeans and sighed. Talk about inflated ego. When had hers gotten so big that she'd have even the passing thought he was interested in her. He was too busy worrying about his precious image. Business dinner, he'd said. Probably wanted to coach her on what to say in case the reporters came back. He didn't give a flip about her.

Which was fine. Just peachy. That made tonight easier. She'd stuff her face with the smoked ribs and baked beans Ella was famous for, then sneak out.

She gathered up the fresh under things and white shirt she'd laid out on the bed, and was about to head for the shower when she noticed the folded-up piece of paper Jessica had given her. She had forgotten about it, then almost missed it when it blended into the patchwork quilt.

After setting her clothes aside again, she picked up the small square and started to unfold it. Quickly she realized that it was a newspaper clipping, and her heart sank. True, she'd briefly wished she had a copy of the picture, but ultimately she had decided against it. What she didn't understand was why Rose would send this to her.

Tempted to simply toss it into the trash without looking at it, she hesitated until a sudden overwhelming need had her unfolding it the rest of the way.

She stared openmouthed at the photo from today's paper.

Shay had just punched Corky Higgins in his big fat nose. Beneath it the caption read, Prince Sharif Al Farid–El Jeved Slays Dragon For His Ladylove.

Chapter Eight

"Well, don't you look sharp." Jessica sashayed across the pool deck to circle Livy while giving her the once-over.

"Knock it off, Jess." Livy glanced nervously around the crowd of at least two dozen people. Fortunately everyone was talking and laughing and paying no attention to them. "And don't get any big ideas. The only reason I wore this dress is because it gives me more room for Ella's smoked ribs and peach cobbler."

"Of course." Jessica grinned. "Why would I think anything else?"

"Okay. I'm outta here." She turned to go, but Jessica looped an arm through hers.

"Come on, Livy, I'll be good. There's a margarita over here with your name on it, then we'll circulate."

Normally Livy didn't drink anything stronger than sweetened iced tea, but right now, a margarita sounded awfully good. After seeing that picture of Shay decking Corky, her thoughts were all a jumble again. Not that she actually thought Shay had defended her honor. Corky had a way of saying things that got a person riled. But she sure didn't mind that some folks might think that way. It made her feel less foolish.

Maybe even a little special.

Which made her an even bigger fool.

Anxious for that margarita suddenly, she let Jessica lead her to the bar where Rocky, one of the other hands, played bartender for the night. Livy hadn't seen him since yesterday, before the first newspaper had come out, and she braced herself for a smart-aleck remark, or at the very least, a disapproving look. She received neither.

Of course Rocky was always happy acting as bartender. She suspected he guzzled half as much as he poured.

Still, his lack of reaction helped her to relax somewhat as she slowly sipped her tart salty drink and followed Jessica around. And kept a furtive lookout for Shay. But several more couples from neighboring ranches had arrived, and with the thickening crowd, it was becoming more difficult to see.

One thing about the Colemans—they spared no energy or expense in throwing a party, no matter how last-minute it was. Lanterns had been strung across the balconies off the upstairs bedrooms that overlooked the courtyard, as well as the back patio, where off to the side, steaks and ribs sizzled on large half-barrel grills. Stretched across two of the stone arches was a banner that read It's A Girl.

Even the moonlight reflecting off the lake overlooked by the house appeared to have been made-to-order. Its glow seemed almost otherworldly, and the air, scented with Ella's mouthwatering grilled meats and corn, promised a taste of heaven.

"Do you know what time we're eating?" Livy asked suddenly.

Jessica's eyebrows shot up. "Because you're hun-

gry?'' A slow, teasing smile curved her mouth. ''Or
are you trying to figure out when you can sneak
away?''

''Actually, you know I'm not used to drinking, and
on an empty stomach…''

''Say no more.'' Jessica started to leave, stopped and
lifted the half-empty glass out of Livy's hand. ''Stay
here. I'll be right back.''

That was fine with Livy. She found a table to lean
on and watched her friend make her way toward the
food still in the midst of preparation. It wasn't as if she
were close to fainting or anything, but she did feel sort
of light-headed.

More people had arrived, some of them Desert Rose
boarders who stayed on the property while Stanley Fox,
a part-time employee, helped them train their horses
for showing.

One of the boarders stood out in particular. Even in
jeans, Savannah looked quite stunning, but tonight, in
a short white denim dress, she was amazing. Several
male heads turned as she walked across the patio.

Including Randy Coleman, Vi's husband.

Livy stared as he immediately excused himself from
his conversation with Hal Grover, one of the other
hands and Ella's husband. Randy met the striking bru-
nette halfway, then steered her toward the bar, the two
of them laughing over something she said in his ear.

They were talking business, of course. Savannah had
an Arabian boarded at the Desert Rose that showed
enormous potential. Besides, Randy and Vi were the
perfect happily married couple. But Vi had been awfully moody lately. Gosh, Livy hoped Savannah wasn't
the reason.

Livy hated the direction in which her thoughts were

going and turned away from the couple. She peered through the crowd trying to locate Jessica. It took only seconds to spot her. She was talking to Shay.

At the sight of him, Livy's entire body tensed and her chest tightened almost painfully. She glanced around to see if anyone was watching her watch him, but everyone appeared to be wrapped up in their own conversations.

Slowly she swung her gaze back to Shay. He was smiling at Jess, his head tilted slightly to the side, totally absorbed in what she was saying.

Something jolted Livy. It seemed almost physical, like a sudden attack of stomach flu, squeezing her insides, forming a lump in her throat the size of Austin.

She closed her eyes and gripped the table tighter, trying to steady herself. Nothing else happened. When she opened her eyes again and her gaze fixed on Jessica's thick mane of beautiful auburn hair, the way her upturned face seemed captivated by Shay, Livy realized, with equal amounts of shock, shame and disgust, what was going on. She wasn't sick. No physical ailment had suddenly assaulted her.

She was jealous. Of Jessica and Shay.

They made a striking couple, and with Jess's fancy college education and her history of traveling, they probably had a lot in common. The thought made Livy feel a little sick after all.

Horrified at her reaction, she straightened and watched helplessly as Jessica started back in her direction, alone, a plate of food in her hands.

"You look awful," Jess said, as she slid the plate onto the table, her anxious gaze fastened on Livy. "I brought you some cheese and crackers and fruit. That should hold you over."

"Thanks, but I was thinking maybe I'd better just go lie down." It was the perfect opportunity to duck out since Jess thought she looked ill. "I'll come back later if I'm up to it."

Suspicion briefly narrowed Jessica's gaze. She pulled out a chair. "Sit and have a bite to eat first, and maybe it'll pass."

"I don't know…"

"Come on. You shouldn't try walking all the way to the bunkhouse right now. Besides, I told my cousin we'd be here for a while. He has to make a phone call, then if you have to go, he can walk you back."

"Your cousin?"

Jess looked at her funny. "Yeah, you know… Sharif."

Livy blinked. "He's your cousin."

"Of course, he's my cousin." Jess frowned. "He's Alex's, Mac's and Cade's brother."

Livy shook her head, half laughing. How much more foolish could she feel? Of course, they were cousins. And Livy was the village idiot. Sheesh!

"Here, eat some of this cheese. You're scaring me."

"*I'm* scaring me." Livy sighed.

What was wrong with her? She'd read too many fairy tales lately, that's what. It didn't matter if Jess and Shay were cousins, or not. Livy meant nothing to Shay. Even though he had punched out Corky Higgins. For all she knew, Corky had made a crack about how Shay had been slumming. Any offense taken by Shay would have been on his own behalf. Not hers.

"Hey, look who's here."

Livy looked in the direction of Jessica's gaze and saw neighboring rancher, Cord Brannigan, shaking hands with Alex. After Shay, Cord was one of the most handsome men Livy had ever met. Even if he did want to buy Prince from her. Which would never happen in a million years.

"Can you believe he brought that woman with him?" Jessica whispered. "She sure doesn't look happy to be here."

Livy grunted to herself. That made two of them. "Why shouldn't he bring his sister?"

"Oh, please, don't be so naive."

Nibbling a piece of sharp cheddar, Livy peered thoughtfully at Cord and the woman. When she'd arrived two months ago out of the blue, Cord had taken her in and introduced her as his sister from back East. With his black hair and hazel eyes contrasting her long blond ponytail and baby blues, the rumors had started immediately.

Besides, as far as anyone knew, Cord had always lived in Texas. Next to the Colemans, he had one of the largest ranches this side of Austin. No one really believed she was his sister, but Cord wasn't the type of man who needed to explain himself. And folks around Bridle wouldn't dare ask him to.

"Cord's about thirty-four. How old would you say she is?" Jessica asked, and reached for a cracker. "Younger than us, for sure. Twenty, maybe?"

"Probably about that. Want me to ask her for you? Looks like they're coming this way."

"You wouldn't!" Jessica nearly choked on the cracker, then made a face at Livy's teasing grin. "I can tell you're feeling better."

"A little," she said with a noncommittal shrug, and kept her gaze on Cord and his sister as they made their way across the patio, stopping occasionally to chat a minute.

But it wasn't really them Livy was trying to keep an eye on.

She was still nervous about seeing Shay, especially out in public like this. Being with Jessica would make it easier. She hoped.

"Good evening, Livy, Jess."

Startled, Livy's gaze flew to Cord, and she smiled politely as he tipped his hat to them. She tried to slow down her pounding heart. She'd been so caught up in trying to find Shay, she'd lost track of Cord and his sister.

"You both look especially pretty tonight," he said, and snatched a piece of cheese off the plate.

"You're looking pretty hunky yourself, Cord. Doing anything later?" Jess asked, and he laughed.

Livy chuckled softly and slid a look at Cord's sister. Her eyes had widened at Jessica's brassy remark, and then a shy grin tugged at her mouth.

Cord turned to take her hand and draw her into the circle. "Don't mind Jess," he said. "She still hasn't forgiven me for not asking her to the senior prom. But she *was* only eight. You two have met my sister, Brianna, right?"

Jessica rolled her eyes. "I may have been only eight, but he did ask me because no one else would go with him." Then she smiled at the younger woman and pulled out a chair. "Hi, Brianna. We met last month at the grocery store. Want to sit with us for a while?"

Brianna looked tentatively at Cord, who nodded, then she took the seat. Jessica pushed the plate of cheese and fruit toward her and immediately engaged her in conversation.

Cord didn't look the least bit concerned, even though it was well-known around Bridle that Jessica could pry a secret out of a monk if she put her mind to it. Instead, he focused his entire attention on Livy, and gave her the smile that had once had the power to make her knees weak.

"So, how's my favorite gelding doing?" He pulled out the chair next to Livy and, straddling it, faced her. "I'm sure you're taking good care of him."

Livy laughed. "Prince is just fine, thank you. And he's quite happy right where he is."

"I assume you're riding him next week."

"At the annual Breakneck Race? You bet. I hope you won't mind coming in second."

Amusement curved his mouth. "I'm not sure I'm entering this year. Brianna and I have something to take care of back East. I just want to make sure you don't let anything happen to my horse."

He looked so serious suddenly it gave Livy the willies. She didn't understand his single-minded desire to own Prince. He was one of the richest men in the county, able to afford any horse he wanted. But he sure as hell wasn't going to get hers.

She saw someone waving at them and inclined her head in that direction. "Looks like Hal Grover's trying to get your attention."

Cord glanced over his shoulder, then stood. "We have some business to discuss, if you'll excuse me."

Brianna stood, too, her eagerness to stick with him plain.

He didn't encourage her to stay, only gave her a brief smile before saying to Livy, "I admire your instinct in buying Prince when he was still a runt. You're a smart horsewoman, and a good trainer. But one of these days he's going to get to be too much for you. And I'll be first in line with my checkbook."

She didn't say anything as he walked away, Brianna keeping pace with him. He was so wrong, he didn't even deserve a response.

Jess growled. "Don't let him get to you. I don't know what's the matter with him. He never used to be so pompous and stubborn. In fact, he and Alex used to be really good friends. But a few years ago, Cord went to Houston for a month, for God knows what, and he's never been the same since."

Livy shrugged. "He doesn't bother me. Prince is staying right where he is. Cord can go hound somebody else."

Jessica leaned back in her chair, a mysterious smile on her face. "That's okay. He served his purpose tonight."

"What are you talking about?"

Jess looked past her. "You'll see in about ten seconds." When Livy started to turn around to see what she was staring at, Jess said, "I wouldn't do that if I were you."

Out of the corner of her eye, Livy saw Shay coming toward them. "What does he have to do with anything?" she whispered fiercely, her pulse speeding in anticipation when he stopped to pick up a drink.

"Don't tell me there isn't anything going on between you two." Jess shook her head, her eyes twinkling with curiosity and excitement. "Man, when you were tête-à-tête with Cord, I thought Sharif was going to jump out of his skin."

"How do you know? You were talking to Brianna."

"Right. I think she got out two whole sentences." Jess grinned. "Here he comes."

Of course, Jess was wrong. She was probably just trying to get Livy riled. And darn, but it was working.

Livy moistened her lips, shifted in her seat, crossed and uncrossed her legs, stretched them out, then crossed them at the ankles. Why was she suddenly so darn uncomfortable? The metal patio chair felt like a boulder under her fanny.

"Wow, you've got legs!"

Livy jerked her head at the sound of Mickey's voice. Shay stopped five feet behind him. Mickey obviously hadn't seen him.

"Hey, Smith, I don't think I ever saw you in a dress before," Mickey said, frowning as if it was some big puzzle.

Livy wanted to strangle him. She wouldn't even look at Shay. If he seemed the least bit like he was enjoying this, she'd have to strangle him, too. "Yes, you have," she muttered.

"Nope. I would have remembered." He tipped a bottle of beer to his lips.

Livy scrambled for something to say, something to change the subject. She glanced helplessly at Jess.

"I trust you have asked the ladies if they would also like something to drink?" Shay moved in beside Mickey, whose eyes bugged out.

Livy and Jessica both ducked when it looked as though he might spray them with the sip he'd taken.

But he swallowed, then cleared his throat. "I was just about to do that very thing. Ladies?"

Jessica giggled and shook her head.

Livy thought about saying something to make him squirm, but took pity on him when she saw the bead of perspiration forming over his right eyebrow. "No, thanks." She pointed to the barbecue area. "I think Hal is trying to get your attention."

Mickey gave her a grateful smile, then scampered away without another word.

"I hope I did not interrupt." Shay took the chair Cord had occupied and swung it around to face the table. He placed it awfully close to Livy, and she glanced around to see if anyone was watching them. But Hannah, Alex's very pregnant wife, had just arrived and quickly became the center of attention.

"Not at all," Jessica said, "we've been waiting for you, haven't we?"

Livy met her friend's mischievous eyes and sent her a silent warning signal, wishing she was in kicking distance. "I think I'll go see Hannah while you two visit. I haven't seen her in a while."

"Do you think you should get up yet? Do you feel well enough?"

Shay turned sharply in Livy's direction.

Darn that Jess. "Good as new." She smiled brightly and scooted her chair back.

Shay laid a hand on her arm. "If you are ill, perhaps I should accompany you."

His touch made Livy all tingly and warm and boneless. Jess had just made her list of people to be strangled.

Jessica stood abruptly, pretending to be distracted by something. Livy knew she was pretending, because Jess always nibbled her lower lip when she fibbed. Just like she was doing now. "You know, I don't think it was Mickey who Hal wanted. He seems to be calling for me."

"Knock it off, Jess," Livy warned, but her friend only winked as she scampered away.

Sighing, Livy turned to Shay. He looked awfully serious. When she tried to move her arm, his grip tightened slightly.

"You are ill?" he asked, the obvious concern in his face taking her aback.

"Not exactly. I had a margarita and I'm not used to alcohol."

His gaze lowered to the plate of half-eaten food. "Ah, I understand." He picked up a piece of cheese and brought it to her lips. "Then you should have more food in your stomach."

Livy's breath caught. Thank goodness, it had started getting dark. But not dark enough that she couldn't see his eyes. Intense, bold, tempting, they demanded her complete attention, her surrender.

She reared her head back slightly, then took the cheese from him with her fingers. "Thank you."

He smiled and gave her a small nod. "That man with whom you were speaking earlier, is he a boarder?"

At his strained tone, a thrill shot through her. Could Jess have been right? "He has a large spread next door."

"Perhaps he would like you to work for him? He seemed very eager for your attention."

His fishing around pleased her far more than it should have, and it briefly occurred to her to string him along. But she wasn't good at that sort of thing. He'd see through her in a minute. "Oh, he's eager, all right. He wants to buy Prince."

Shay frowned. "So, I have a rival."

She stared at him, her jaw slackening at his bold remark.

He studied her face, his expression unreadable. "If you ever decide to sell him, I would like first consideration."

Prince. He meant he was a rival for Prince. Not her. Embarrassed at her mistaken notion, she looked away and murmured, "You're both out of luck. He'll never be for sale. Not ever."

"So you have said." He gave her an annoying smile that implied he didn't believe her. "You have not eaten your cheese."

"Aren't you afraid to sit here alone with me?"

He looked a little startled at her question. "Why? Do you have unsavory designs on my body?"

"You sure have a weird way of saying things. I meant, it must look bad. People will wonder."

Amusement lit his eyes. "Have you not seen today's paper? I am sure opinions have already been concluded."

At the mention of the picture of him decking Corky, she shifted uncomfortably. "I saw it."

"I doubt this man will give you any more trouble."

"You punched Corky because of me?"

His eyebrows drew together. "You seem surprised."

"I—I didn't think…" She shrugged helplessly.

"He spoke untruths about you that I could not ignore." He raised his chin at a haughty angle, his eyes turning a fierce color.

Flushing with elation, she gave him a shy smile. "You didn't have to do that. King Zak must be furious."

He waved a dismissive hand. "My father understands the importance of defending a lady's honor."

That sounded impersonal, and some of her excitement faded. "I can take care of myself."

"A most admirable quality in a woman, I am coming to believe," he said with a slight bow, and she got all warm and fuzzy again. His expression turned serious.

"Tell me, Olivia, how have the others been treating you?"

"I haven't really seen them much." Surprised that she'd forgotten they were probably the object of gossip even now, her gaze quickly swept the crowd. Mickey was eyeing them, and so was Jessica. But no one else.

"I do not want you to have to avoid your friends and co-workers. Tell me how to make things right for you."

His earnestness touched her. "It wasn't your fault." She stared down at her clasped hands. "If I hadn't kissed you back, the picture couldn't have been taken."

He nudged her chin up. "You regret kissing me?"

She could lie and say yes. But that was difficult to do while looking him straight in the eyes. "No," she whispered. "None of it."

"Hey, everyone, the new father is here!" someone yelled, and everyone turned toward the house.

An unlit cigar stuck out from the middle of Mac's big grin as he came out the back door. His hands were fisted around cigars and suckers, which he immediately passed out. Jessica was the first to grab a cigar.

Livy laughed. "Come on, let's go congratulate him." When Shay hesitated, she automatically reached for his hand. "Come on, *Uncle* Shay."

At his stunned look, she instantly released him. Although she'd grabbed his hand impulsively and wished she hadn't, she didn't see what the big deal was since he'd touched her so many times. Maybe in his country that was too forward a thing for a woman to do.

He frowned, his expression one of total bewilderment. "Uncle?"

She nodded. "You're Mac's brother. That makes you little Sarah's uncle."

"Of course." His expression started to clear and a beautiful smile curved his mouth. "I am an uncle."

She laughed at the awe in his voice. "Isn't it exciting?"

"Yes, I suppose it is." The old reserve edged back in.

"Oh, come on, you can be a softy. Nobody will notice." She started across the patio and he fell into step beside her, taking her hand.

She thought about pulling away after having stopped to consider the possible consequences, but what the heck? After the two newspaper photographs, how much damage could a little hand-holding do? In fact, wouldn't it just surprise everyone to know that Shay actually didn't mind being seen with her.

Her head held a little higher, she walked alongside him to where Mac, surrounded by well-wishers, passed out the cigars and strawberry suckers. As soon as Mac saw his brother, he broke from the crowd and embraced Shay with a big hug.

She let go of his hand and stood back, watching with interest the unguarded display of emotion in Shay's face. At first, he seemed at a loss, unprepared for Mac's open show of affection. But then he relaxed, and the look of absolute contentment that softened his features was almost indescribable.

Livy had to look away. Her heart constricted with joy for him, and a yearning she hadn't felt in a long time.

She noticed Vi standing off to the side and grateful for the distraction, stepped back to chat with her. But Vi tensed as soon as Livy got close and briefly turned away, sniffing.

"Wow, you look really nice," Livy said, meaning

it. She'd only seen the older woman in a dress a couple of times, and the lavender sheath she wore this evening showed off her tanned arms and beautiful red hair.

"Not bad for a grandmother, I guess," Vi said, and sniffed. "Well, adopted grandmother. But the fact is, I'm old enough to be one." Her gaze drifted to where Randy stood with Savannah.

Livy bit her lip, wanting to say something, anything to comfort Vi, but she just didn't know what to say. She still didn't believe there was anything beyond business going on between Randy and the attractive boarder, but she knew better than to bring up *that* subject.

Vi straightened suddenly. "Is something wrong with Hannah?"

Not waiting for Livy to reply, she rushed toward Alex's wife, who held her pregnant stomach, a frightened look on her face.

Just as they got to her side, Hannah's apprehension disappeared and she smiled broadly. "One of them kicked," she said, frantically waving Alex to her. "One of the babies kicked."

Alex was there in an instant, his expression one of total awe as he held a palm against her belly. "That one's a boy. No doubt about it."

Everyone laughed.

Vi sniffed, and Livy reached over and squeezed her hand. Her gaze briefly swept the crowd until it connected with Shay's. He winked, and something fluttered in her chest.

"Excuse me, everyone. Can I have your attention?" Cade cleared his throat and slipped an arm around his wife's waist. "Serena and I have some news. We were going to save it, but you all know how I hate my brothers upstaging me.''

Mac, his twin, snorted, and several others joined him in calling out smart-aleck comments.

Cade laughed good-naturedly, then raised a silencing hand. His gaze went to Rose, who had just stepped outside carrying a platter of biscuits. He smiled at her, and then at Vi. ''Not to be outdone, Serena and I are going to make both my moms grandmothers again.'' He paused. ''We're having twins.''

Livy could tell Vi was touched. As the woman who had raised Cade, she was glad to have been included. But she looked so overwhelmed, Livy's heart went out to her.

Rose, however, nearly dropped the platter in her haste to hug Cade and Serena. King Zak rescued the biscuits, but he looked a little dazed himself. And then Livy remembered he was Serena's father. Her twins would be his first grandchildren.

To her amazement, Livy found herself sniffing. Serena and Hannah both looked so radiant, and their husbands were beaming, and everyone seemed so darn happy, the air almost crackled with it. Vi headed for Serena, but Livy stayed back. It was family time, she figured. She'd offer her congratulations later. Crossing her arms, she hugged herself against an unexpected chill. Her gaze found Shay's once more. He'd been watching her again.

''I have something else to say.'' Cade waved for everyone's attention. After he got it, he looked directly at Shay. ''Well, little brother, you're the only one left who hasn't bitten the dust,'' he said, grinning, and got punched in the arm by Serena. ''It's your turn. When are we going to hear some news from you?''

Everyone fell silent. Anyone who hadn't heard the rumors or seen the newspaper or had been told outright sure knew about Shay now. The only sound Livy could hear was the steaks sizzling on the grill, the blood rushing to her ears. Several people looked from Shay to her. She swallowed hard and slowly shrank back into the shadows. Her gaze briefly darted to him, but he seemed to be avoiding her eyes.

He smiled at Cade. ''I believe you Americans have a saying which expresses my thoughts well on the matter. Hell will freeze over before I have *that* kind of news.''

Livy hadn't realized she'd been holding her breath until it came out in a rush. Even though she had no right to the emotions, disappointment and sadness swamped her.

While everyone laughed and goaded Shay, she cursed her stupidity and backed deeper into the shadows. What had she expected from the man? For goodness' sake, she'd only known him two days. But with Shay, she had a feeling it wouldn't matter if it had been two years. She wasn't his type. Never would be.

He might not be the prince for her, but she did have a Prince waiting in the stables. When she was sure no one was watching, she turned and ran.

Chapter Nine

Sharif slipped away from the festivities as soon as he could do so without attracting attention. Even though Livy had at least a twenty-minute head start, he had a fairly good idea where she had gone.

When he arrived at the stables, Prince was gone and Livy was nowhere in sight. That surprised him. He had figured she might be talking to Prince, not taking a moonlight ride.

He walked outside and squinted at the horizon, then toward the lake where the trees cast long shadows. There was sufficient moonlight to see, and there was no sign of her.

Rubbing the tension at the back of his neck, his gaze tracked the frenzied movement of a squirrel. It would be insane to try to follow Livy. He had no idea which way she had chosen to ride. The terrain was unfamiliar to him, as were the horses. And he was not dressed properly.

He let out a curse that sent the squirrel scurrying up the drainage pipe that ran down the side of the stable. Then he went back inside and selected a brown Morgan. Fortunately the tack room was unlocked, so he did not have to break in. He studied the various saddles for a moment, found a suitable one and hoisted it off the rack.

Along the far wall hung a wide assortment of bridles. He stared at them for a moment, trying to make a decision, and it suddenly occurred to him that he had never before saddled his own horse. He was unsure whether he knew how.

A week ago it would not have mattered to him. Now the thought was staggering. Amazingly difficult to digest. But it was the sad truth, and he picked out a snaffle bridle without confidence.

"You sure you want to use that one?" Alex asked from behind.

His approach had been silent, and Sharif stiffened as his brother moved up alongside him. "Were you not enjoying the party?"

Alex smiled. "I was wondering the same thing about you. And then I figured it out." He lifted a bridle off the wall, briefly frowned at it, before returning it and selecting another. "Try this one."

Sharif begrudgingly accepted the bridle. As much as he hated being shown up, he would never endanger a horse. Alex would know which would be the most appropriate tack. He wondered what else Alex thought he knew. However, he left the question unspoken.

"Do you even know in which direction she rode off?" Alex picked up the saddle and headed toward the stalls.

Sharif grunted. Were all big brothers so inquisitive?

"If you don't, I think I do." Alex heaved the saddle over a wooden rack near the Morgan's stall.

Sharif stared warily at him. "How would you know this?"

"Because getting ready for the race next week is how she spends all her free time."

"What sort of race?"

"We have a tradition around here. It's called the annual Breakneck Race. Most of the ranchers and hands throw in—"

"Breakneck?" Sharif sincerely hoped he misunderstood.

"It's not quite as bad as it sounds." Alex shrugged. "The terrain is pretty rough, but don't worry—Livy's a competent rider and she's got a damn good horse."

"I cannot believe you allow her to participate in something so dangerous."

Alex chuckled. "When you get to know her better, you'll understand that it's not a matter of allowing, or not allowing, Livy Smith to do anything. And I suggest you not let her hear you say anything like that again."

Angry and at a loss for words, Sharif had snatched the bridle and started to enter the stall, when Alex put a hand on his shoulder. The tension wondrously fled from his body. It was an odd sensation, an unexpected humbling one, to know this was his brother, connected to him by blood, someone who wanted nothing from him as prince of Balahar. Someone who offered friendship and love, and asked for nothing.

"Was I that obvious?" Sharif asked without looking at him.

Alex squeezed his shoulder, then dropped his hand. "Probably not to most, but Cade and I guessed. Mac would have, too, but he's too busy passing out cigars."

It was an amazing thing that Sharif did not have to explain what he meant. His brother knew he had been referring to Olivia. The thought warmed him. One side of his mouth automatically lifted. "And you, big brother, will be busy passing out cigars soon, too."

Surprised gleamed in Alex's eyes, and then a slow grin curved his lips. Being called "big brother" had clearly pleased him. "Yup. I can't wait." He paused, and his smile faltered. "Can I talk you out of going after her?"

Sharif shook his head.

"You could get lost and have to spend the night on the lumpy ground, while she's snug back here in the bunkhouse."

"That is possible."

"You're as stubborn as she is. You two just might deserve each other." With a half smile, Alex helped him saddle the Morgan. "Don't plan on changing her mind. She wants that prize money for something, and she seems pretty determined to win."

"I like her," Sharif said out of the blue. "She has strength of character and I admire her dedication to her work and…"

"And she doesn't look bad in a dress," Alex finished with a laugh. "You don't have to explain to me. I like Livy, too. But she's going to be madder than a cornered wildcat when she finds out you followed her."

Sharif climbed onto the horse. "I would be surprised if she reacted in any other manner."

"Follow the trail toward the lake. When it forks, take the right one. If we don't see you by morning, I'll come looking."

"I will return before midnight."

Alex stepped aside. "Good luck then."

"Alex?" He paused. "Thank you."

Again, pleasure lit the other man's eyes. "No problem. That's what big brothers are for."

Sharif gently tugged on the reins and nudged the horse into motion, a whirlwind of emotions swirling inside him.

"By the way," Alex called out, and Sharif looked over his shoulder at him. "If you want to keep up with Livy, I suggest you learn how to do things for yourself."

THERE WAS NOTHING BETTER in the whole world than riding, as far as Livy was concerned. Even her first horse, Chimney Sweep, who'd been nothing more than a broken-down nag donated to the orphanage when Livy was thirteen, gave her more pleasure than any human being ever could.

She remembered having begged Father Michael for two solid weeks to keep Chimney Sweep. And when he'd finally agreed, but only if Livy promised to take sole responsibility for her, Livy hadn't given the vow a second thought. From that day forward, Livy had never disappointed the mare, and she had never disappointed Livy.

The same thing couldn't be said for most people, she thought as she guided Prince to the edge of the lake. Friendships and love were almost always conditional, depending on what someone wanted from you.

Prince wasn't like that. All he wanted was feed, some sugar now and then, and lots of exercise. She reached down to stroke his neck and he stretched back for more.

"You thirsty, boy?" She hopped down and led him closer to the water before dropping the reins.

In the eerie quiet, his noisy slurps echoed off the

trees and made her smile. She sank to the ground and hugged her bent knees, watching him, contentment swelling in her heart.

This was her life. One she'd made for herself. One that gave her so many daily pleasures. She didn't need anyone. Certainly no snooty prince who treated people like playthings.

Sighing, she picked a long blade of grass and stuck it in the corner of her mouth. The shimmering silver moonlight reflecting off the water soothed her wounded spirit, and she lay back on the grass to stare at the stars. No palace with all the gold in the world could compete with a clear Texas night, she decided. If she ever had a daughter, she wouldn't read her any fairy tales about a Prince Charming sweeping the hapless young girl off her feet. Life didn't work that way.

Livy closed her eyes and breathed in the crisp night air. That's what had gotten her into trouble. Hoping some tall, dark, handsome man would whisk her away, and give her a home and name. Well, Smith was just fine, and the Desert Rose was more than she could've hoped for. But there was something else she wanted...

Watching Mac pass out cigars with that goofy grin on his face had been a jolt. And the way Serena glowed when Cade announced they were expecting twins had started Livy's heart fluttering. Funny, she hadn't really thought much about having kids before, but she had tonight.

She hauled herself up to a sitting position when it sounded as though Prince had about drunk his fill. And before her mind started weaving any more fantasies. Shay had made it pretty plain about how he felt.

"Olivia!"

Shay's voice came from somewhere on the south

side of the lake. Startled, she straightened and listened, trying to gauge how far away he was. How in the heck had he found her?

Slowly, quietly, she climbed to her feet and dusted off the back of her sundress. She hadn't stopped to change. She hadn't expected to run into anyone out here.

After listening a moment longer, and hearing nothing, she decided he wasn't so close that she couldn't ride away without being seen. Or caught.

"Olivia, Prince, are you here?"

Oh, hell. She watched Prince's ears perk up, and knew what came next. His loud whinny bounced off the trees. After a few seconds of silence and indecision, she scrambled for the reins.

"Olivia, stay where you are."

"Yeah, right," she mumbled, and swung into the saddle. She didn't know if he could see her or not, but if he could, he'd probably just gotten an eyeful of hot-pink panties. But she didn't care. All she wanted was to get as far away from him as possible.

"Come on, Prince, let's go." She nudged him and they took off down the path that led through the trees to the south pasture.

"Olivia! What the devil are you doing?" Shay called, sounding closer than she'd counted on.

Obviously she was also in his line of vision. She urged Prince to speed up and they galloped through the pines without looking back.

The thick foliage was a mixed blessing. Although it provided an excellent cover, it also blocked the moonlight, and Livy was forced to slow down. Not only did she not want to endanger Prince, but it occurred to her that if Shay tried to follow, his unfamiliarity with the path would put him at risk.

She muttered a curse. The smart thing to do would be to stop. As irritated as she was with him, she'd never forgive herself if Shay or his horse were injured.

Slowing Prince down, she was about to call out to Shay when Prince stumbled. A second before, she had relaxed her hand and now she lost her grip and struggled for a hold. Panicked, Prince reared slightly, enough for her to slide backward, off the saddle and onto a stump.

The jagged bark scraped her bare thighs and, when she bounced to the side, her head made contact with a tree just as a sharp pain shot through her ankle. She sucked in a breath at the intensity of the blow, tears springing to her eyes.

When she tried to stand, the pain in her ankle was so acute, she dropped back to the ground. Trees swam before her eyes. Her head throbbed.

"Oh, Prince." She gingerly crawled toward him, praying he hadn't been hurt.

He pranced nervously, but he seemed fine. She studied the impact of each hoof for a moment, then let out a sigh of relief, causing every muscle in her body to smart.

Rolling over onto her back, she stared up at the patches of sky through the trees, waiting for her vision to clear. A slight vibration rose from the ground, the unmistakable pounding of hooves that told her Shay was coming.

She tried to tug her dress over her thighs, but the effort seemed too much, so she stretched back out again, closed her eyes and waited.

"Olivia."

The pounding stopped only a few feet away. She was lucky he hadn't trampled her. She opened her eyes. Things were still a little blurry, but she saw that Shay was riding Chocolate, one of her favorite Morgans. She smiled and closed her eyes again.

"Olivia?" Shay was instantly kneeling beside her, his hand gently touching hers. "Can you speak?"

She took a deep breath and lifted her heavy lids. "Big jerk. You shouldn't have followed me."

His sigh of relief fanned warm breath across her cheeks. "Tell me what hurts."

"Help me up." She hated asking, but she knew that was the only way she could get to her feet.

"Not until we determine your injuries."

"This isn't my first fall, and it won't be my last." She tried to push herself off the ground, and was almost glad when he put a gentle but firm hand on her shoulder.

She wouldn't have made it up by herself, but he didn't have to know that.

"This is no time to be stubborn." He brought his face level with hers and stared into her eyes. She blinked away the pain-induced tears. "Tell me so we can get Prince back to his stall. He seems upset."

That was low, using Prince like that. But he was right. "I hit my head." She touched the tender spot and winced. Already a lump was forming. "And my ankle may be sprained."

"How is your vision?"

"Awful. I can still see you."

A brief smile touched his lips. "Anything else I should know before I move you?"

"Yeah, I'm going to wring your neck." She winced

again as he slid an arm beneath her. "When I can do it properly."

"I look forward to your being well enough to do so." He shifted his weight, preparing to lift her. "Ready?"

She curled an arm around his neck and leaned against his broad chest. "Ready."

It wasn't too bad until she tried to move her ankle. Sharp shooting pain had her pressing her lips together to keep from crying out. She glanced down to check for swelling and gasped at how high her dress had ridden up her thigh. Another inch and he could see her tonsils.

"What? Did I hurt you?" Shay froze, and she felt his heart pound against her breast.

"No." She freed a hand and pushed at the material bunched near the leg of her panties. "I should have stopped to change," she mumbled.

"I will make sure you are covered. No one will see you." He lifted her onto the saddle, then gathered Prince's reins.

"You will."

He didn't respond, only climbed up behind her, then gently urged her to lie against his chest.

There was a certain advantage to being small, she realized. Like being able to snuggle between him and the saddle horn without getting too terribly squashed. In fact, under other circumstances, it would have felt rather nice, being cradled in his arms, having the strong, steady beat of his heart against her skin.

Oh, heck, it felt nice now. As long as she didn't jerk her head or move her leg.

"Comfortable?"

She nodded, then regretted it. "Thank you."

"Tell me if you need to stop." He made a clicking sound and Chocolate moved forward.

The mare was well trained and obedient, but Livy had never taught her to respond to any such noise. Shay obviously had a way with horses. Livy didn't know why that should surprise her.

"Everything all right?" he asked several minutes later.

In spite of her certainty that her head was about to split open, she chuckled. "You sound like a mother hen. I'll let you know if anything is wrong."

"Something is wrong. You are too quiet."

"Very funny." She let out a slow breath. Even though they were practically crawling, she felt every hoof-fall. "You wouldn't have any aspirin on you?"

"We will call for the doctor as soon as we get back to the ranch."

"Oh, no." She started to straighten. No way. Painfully, she was forced to relax against him again. "I don't need a doctor. I need two aspirin and a good night's sleep." She paused, and he said nothing. "And probably crutches for a couple of days."

He still didn't say anything, which annoyed the heck out of her. His silence could mean agreement, but she doubted it.

"Drop me off at the bunkhouse. I'll ask Mickey to take care of the horses."

"You will sleep at the main house tonight."

"I will not."

"You likely have a concussion. After the doctor sees you, we will discuss the situation."

Livy gritted her teeth. "I will make my own decisions, thank you very much."

"You are not thinking straight." His chin brushed

the top of her head, and he shifted slightly so that her body sank impossibly deeper against his. "You should never have been riding in the dark. You were very lucky I was there."

"Are you kidding? If you hadn't been chasing me I wouldn't have had the accident."

"You were running from me?"

"Duh."

He fell silent again, and she couldn't tell if he was angry or just didn't understand the term "duh."

"Why would you run from me?" he finally asked, surprise in his voice.

"Why did you follow me?"

He didn't answer, but his heartbeat had picked up speed.

Livy was usually fairly comfortable with silence, but after they'd covered another mile without saying a word, she cleared her throat. "How's Prince doing back there?"

Shay glanced over his shoulder. "He is worried about you."

She smiled. "He doesn't have to be. I'm a pretty tough cookie." She tilted her head back a little so that she could see Shay's face. He looked awfully somber. Was he really that worried? "Thanks for taking Prince and me back. Bet you were tempted to leave me and my smart mouth there."

His mouth curved in a slow, heart-stopping smile. "The thought never crossed my mind."

It was hard to remember why she'd been upset with him. His arms and chest felt strong and comforting, and when a cool breeze made her shiver, he tightened his arms around her, gently, protectively. His warmth made the pain so much more bearable.

Because they traveled slowly, it took over an hour before they could see the lights from the Desert Rose. As they got closer, it was obvious the party had broken up, but a few stragglers sat around the patio, tipping beer bottles.

Livy figured they were probably the Desert Rose gang, because the only thing they liked better than beer was free beer. Which suited her just fine right now. It would be a heck of a lot easier if she could make it to her room without having to explain herself. Or Shay.

Except when they got to the bunkhouse, Shay kept going.

She straightened, painfully. "What are you doing? Stop. You're passing my place."

"I am certain you will be more comfortable in the main house."

"Are you crazy? Haven't we made the front page of the paper enough?"

He steered Chocolate toward the side of the house. "No one will see us. I will take care of everything."

"Oh, sure. You've done such a swell job already." It was horrible feeling so helpless. The only constructive thing she could do was think of ways to get even later. "I'm not seeing the doctor, so if you think bringing me here will—ouch! You did that on purpose."

He glanced down at her. She glared back.

Of course he hadn't jolted them deliberately, and he must have guessed she wasn't seriously hurt by it, because he returned his attention to the path.

"What are you going to do with Prince and Chocolate when we get to the house?"

"I have changed my mind. I like it better when you are silent."

"Tough noogies, and if you don't understand, I'll be

happy to translate.'' Her head still hurt like the dickens, and if she didn't hurry and get some ice on her ankle, she was going to puff up the size of the Goodyear blimp. Any trace of a sense of humor she'd managed to hang on to was slipping fast.

True to his word, he stayed to the left of the house, where no one lingered and few lights were on. He still wouldn't be able to get her into the house without anyone seeing them. And where her final destination would be she hadn't a clue. As far as she could tell, all the spare rooms were full of guests or boarders. Which meant…

He couldn't possibly be taking her to his room.

Her heart just about somersaulted out of her chest at the thought. Surely that wasn't what he had in mind.

''This isn't going to work. Someone will see us,'' she said, when he pulled in the reins and Chocolate came to a stop.

''I will dismount now. Be sure you hold on. Ready?''

Livy sighed. Might as well be talking to a fence post. She braced herself. ''Ready.''

He pulled away from her with the utmost care. When he hopped down, she barely felt so much as a jiggle. But she did miss his warmth, and the solid comfort of his body wrapped around hers.

''Ready?'' he asked again, holding out his arms.

She rearranged her dress, nodded and mentally braced herself for the descent.

It wasn't nearly as bad as she thought it would be. Shay was incredibly patient and gentle as he lifted her down and slowly carried her to the stairs. Not once did he even glance in the vicinity of her exposed thighs, and after he lowered her to the bottom step, he even tugged her hem down.

"I'm too heavy. Take me to the bunkhouse, then you won't have to worry about dragging me upstairs."

"I will only be a moment. Can you stay out of trouble for that long?"

"You're leaving me here?" She tried to push herself up and winced in pain.

He muttered something foreign, then scooped her in his arms again. "From now on," he said, "I will not let you out of my sight."

Chapter Ten

Sharif paced outside the bedroom while Rose got Olivia settled in. The town of Bridle was not so far away. Why had the doctor not arrived yet? Sharif had offered him a handsome enough fee to come to the house. Although he did not understand why he had to do so. In his country, a royal summons was enough.

However, he would have offered much more to have Olivia cared for.

He could not remember ever feeling so panicked or helpless as he did when he saw her lying still on the ground. That in itself was unnerving. He had known her two days. A mere forty-eight hours, yet the turmoil she stirred inside him was startling.

The door opened, and Rose walked out and closed it behind her. She gave him a sympathetic smile. "She's sore, but she'll be fine. Although she's not too happy with you."

He waved a dismissive hand. "Good. Then she is not ailing too badly."

Rose laughed softly. "She sure won't be walking for a while, but the ice has helped keep the swelling down."

"And her head?"

"The aspirin helped, but I'm glad you called the doctor. I'd be surprised if she didn't have a slight concussion."

Sharif pushed a hand through his hair and started to pace again.

"Go ahead," Rose said, and when he looked at her, she winked. "Go in and talk to her."

"Is it safe?"

Rose laughed. "Probably not."

He nodded, and smiled. "Thank you."

"I'm glad you came to me."

Sharif said nothing, he merely nodded again. He was unsure why he had sought her out. He could have gone to Alex. That may have been simpler, since his brother knew he had gone after Olivia. But for some inexplicable reason, it had seemed so natural to go to Rose.

"I'll bring the doctor up when he gets here. If either of you need anything, I'll be in the den reading." She headed for the stairs, her slim body wrapped in a too-big pink robe, and he watched her until she disappeared.

She was too thin, probably from so many years of captivity, yet she never complained. And still, she carried herself as regally and poised as any queen.

Unexpectedly, pride warmed him and, unwilling to analyze its source, he knocked on Olivia's door, then opened it before she granted permission.

She looked small and pale in the queen-size bed, her face framed by two enormous pillows, the covers pulled up to her chin. She blinked as though coming out of a trance, then made a face. "I'm not seeing any stinking doctor, and I mean it. My foot and head are both fine. Ask Rose."

He entered, unhurried, and sat in the chair beside the bed. "My mother agrees with me."

"The heck she—" Olivia stared at him. "What did you say?"

Sharif's chest tightened, making it difficult to breathe. The words had slipped out mindlessly. "The doctor should arrive at any moment. The sooner he examines you, the sooner we can all get some sleep."

She looked at him in annoying silence, a thoughtful frown drawing her eyebrows together. He tensed. If she tried to discuss his slip of the tongue, he would leave immediately.

Indecision gleamed in her eyes, and then she said, "As far as I'm concerned, everyone can go to bed right now. I've seen a doctor once, and that was enough."

"Once? Surely you have been to a doctor—"

She vigorously shook her head, then grimaced, put two fingers to her temple and lay back against the pillow. "Please," she whispered. "Don't do this to me."

This had nothing to do with stubbornness, he suddenly realized. Fear darkened her eyes, made her voice reed thin. He moved the chair closer and took her cold, clammy hand. "I truly doubt this is serious. The doctor will only make suggestions for a quicker recovery."

"No, he won't. You don't know old Doc Simpson. He'll think of a reason to give me a shot for something or other."

"Ah, you had a bad experience with this man." He tried not to smile. "Or perhaps it is the needle you do not like."

She shivered. "Don't say that word."

A knock at the door had her eyes so wide with fright, her grip of his hand so desperate, that he was tempted to send the doctor away. "Shall I stay here with you?"

"Please, don't do this."

He touched her face. "I promise I will not let him give you a shot."

"You promise?"

"On my mother's—" King Zak's words came back to him, and he could not say it. "I swear to you on my life."

Another knock.

He brushed his thumb across her lower lip. "All right?"

She sighed. "Sure, let the executioner in."

He gave her a reassuring smile, then quickly kissed her forehead before he opened the door.

The doctor was a much older man, probably close to retirement age, with snow-white hair, a gray beard and a stern expression. He carried a black bag in one hand, and an ivory-colored cane in the other.

He immediately walked into the room, taking long brisk steps, without the help of the cane. Hovering at the door, Rose raised her eyebrows at Sharif.

"Go on to bed," he told her. "I will let the doctor out."

"Maybe I should stay to make sure Livy doesn't need anything else."

"Let me take care of her."

Her gaze held his. "I know you will." She studied his face a moment longer, the same troubled way Queen Nadirah had when, as a child one day, he had gotten lost for several hours. "Good night."

"Sleep well," he said, but she had already started down the hall, so he quietly closed the door and stood aside.

"Well, young lady, I never thought I'd see this day." Dr. Simpson opened his bag and removed a pair of reading glasses. "You must be pretty banged up to want to see me."

"Who said I wanted to see you?"

The doctor chuckled. "Should have figured." He slipped on his spectacles, dug in his bag for a small flashlight, then eyed Sharif. "You must be the young fella who called."

"Yes."

"Are you one of them sheikhs visiting the Colemans I read about in the paper?"

"Your patient is waiting, Doctor." Sharif held on to his temper by a thread. Olivia was obviously terrified, huddled under the covers, her violet eyes huge with apprehension. And the old goat was more concerned with satisfying his curiosity.

"Don't worry. She's not going anywhere." He lifted the covers near her feet and peered over his glasses at her swollen ankle. "Not for a long time. Heavens, you sure whacked this ankle. Good thing you put ice on it."

He probed the area with two arthritic-looking fingers, wincing when Olivia let out a yelp. "Sorry, honey, I'm not trying to hurt you. I just want to make sure nothing is broken."

"It's not," she said. "I've broken a finger, and two toes. This is just a sprain."

At the pained look on her face, Sharif fisted his hands. He knew the doctor was doing what was necessary to properly diagnose her injuries, but he felt so helpless just watching. He would gladly exchange places with her if it were at all possible.

The doctor replaced the covers over her foot, then lowered his head to look her in the eyes. He flipped on the pencil-thin light and lifted one of her eyelids.

She jerked. "Jeez, Doc, you might warn a body that you're gonna start poking and prodding."

"Livy Smith, I swear you are worse than a ten-year-old. Hold still, doggone it."

Sharif walked over to look out the window, partly to give Olivia some privacy, but mostly because he preferred she not see him smile. She was amazingly strong in many ways, and this was a very different side to her.

Staring out at the cloudless night, he realized there was still much he did not know about her. So much more he longed to learn about her life, her goals, her dreams. Such a totally new experience for him, the idea made him uneasy, while at the same time anticipation thrummed in his veins.

It had started earlier at the festivities, with the arrival of Mac, beaming with pride and contentment. Serena's news had been the crowning blow. It was almost impossible to imagine his little sister as a mother. But her blissful glow, when Cade made the announcement, had the power to warm Sharif even now.

Perhaps he was confusing his happiness for them with a false longing within himself. Or perhaps his feelings were real enough that they had touched Olivia, making her run.

"Okay, we're all through here," Dr. Simpson said. Sharif turned from the window just as the man snapped his black bag closed. Olivia was half sitting up, leaning against the mahogany headboard, her face pale and drawn.

"You do like I told you, young lady, and you'll be up and running in no time." He reached into his pocket and held up a red sucker. "All my good patients get one of these."

A reluctant smile lifted her lips, and she took the candy. "Thanks, Doc. For everything."

He smiled kindly, then started for the door. "Get some rest, and I'll leave a prescription for this nice young fella to have filled tomorrow."

"Hey, Doc." She sat up a little straighter. "Could you come here a second?" Her gaze darted to Sharif, and when the doctor approached the bed, she motioned him closer. "Look, Doc, about the bill," she said in a lowered voice that Sharif strained to hear.

Impolite of him, he knew, but she looked so worried he could not do the gentlemanly thing and walk away. If a matter concerned her, he wanted to help.

"I don't have a lot of cash right now, but by next week I'll be in good shape. Can you let me slide until then?"

"You expecting a windfall, are you?" the doctor asked, smiling. "Maybe you plan on winning the Texas lottery?"

"I wish." Livy gave him a sleepy grin. "I'm gonna win the next best thing—the Breakneck Race. You might think about placing a wager on Prince and me. We've been practicing hard, I'd say we've got the race all sewed up."

The doctor snorted. "Maybe that knock in the head you got is worse than I thought. There is no way on God's green earth that you're going to be able to ride in that race. So get that out of your noggin right now."

"You're wrong, Doc." She slowly shook her head, her violet eyes clouding with growing concern as realization sunk in. "I'll be in that race. I have to."

"Sorry, Livy, but that ankle won't be healed enough." He headed back toward the door. "But I'm not going to waste my breath trying to talk you out of it. You try climbing into a saddle and you'll be in too much pain to even give the matter another thought.''

"Wait, Doc.'' Panic crackled in her voice. "You can give me a painkiller or something. Just long enough to get through the race.''

He opened the door and paused. "The only thing that would do the trick comes in the form of a shot.''

She visibly swallowed. "Okay, then…'' Her voice caught. "We'll do that.''

Dr. Simpson smiled kindly. "I was only teasing. What kind of doctor would I be to encourage you to ride with a hurt ankle and minor concussion? I'm afraid you're going to have to wait until next year's race, Livy.''

Her pale and stricken face went blank as she stared off toward the window, and Sharif would have given just about anything to know what she was thinking.

"The bill should be sent to me,'' Sharif said in a low voice as he followed the doctor out of the room. "I will see that it is taken care of immediately.''

Dr. Simpson waved a hand. "No charge. It was worth coming out here just to see Livy.'' He chuckled. "She swore no doctor would ever get near her again. I warned her. Never is a long time.''

Sharif watched the man amble out of the room and down the hall. He looked weary, each step slow and heavy, his shoulders slightly stooped. This time, he used his cane.

"Doctor?''

The older man stopped, and Sharif met him halfway down the hall.

"May I give you a lift home?'' he asked, and the doctor frowned.

"Thanks for the offer, son, but I brought my own car."

"Perhaps if you are too tired to drive—"

Dr. Simpson issued a sound of disgust that was tempered by the twinkle in his eye. "I'm not that old that I need a chauffeur. You go back and console Livy. If I know her, she's still going to want to enter that race. I'd sure hate to see her fall on that hard head of hers again."

Sharif fell into step beside the man. Ironically, he had earlier accused the doctor of inquisitiveness. Now he had this sudden impulse to learn everything the doctor knew about Olivia. "If she never went to see you, how did you get to know Olivia so well?"

"Olivia?" He laughed. "Bet she loves you calling her that. I still run into her at the orphanage now and then. She spends a lot of time with the children, reading to them, that sort of thing. Well, I'd better be saying good-night. I have to be in my office bright and early tomorrow morning."

Sharif held open the front door. "Wait," he said, and reached into his pocket. He pulled out a wad of folded American bills tucked inside a solid gold money clip. "Here, for the house call."

Dr. Simpson stared at the stack of hundreds. "That's an awful lot of money."

He shrugged, truly not knowing how much it was. "Here, Doctor."

"I can't take that. Besides, Livy wouldn't like you paying her bill."

"You misunderstand. This is merely a donation for your favorite charity." Sharif smiled. "The orphanage, perhaps?"

"Well, if you put it that way..." Dr. Simpson pocketed the money. "I'll call Harold at the pharmacy to-morrow with a prescription. Good night."

Sharif waited until the older man had climbed into his dusty Ford pickup and started the engine before he went back upstairs. He knocked softly at Olivia's door and when he received no response, he opened it and peeked inside.

The bed was empty.

LIVY SAT on the tiled bathroom floor, too exhausted and sore and afraid to move. It had taken all her strength and determination to make it this far. She slumped back against the cold stucco wall and closed her eyes. How was she ever going to make it to the race?

She had to think of something. There was no way she could *not* enter that race. The orphanage's roof couldn't withstand another wet winter. Father Michael was counting on her, and she owed him.

Someone knocked softly on the door and she was tempted to keep quiet until they went away. Except she knew it was probably Shay looking for her, and he'd been nothing but kind and patient. Even if he had caused the dang accident.

"Olivia?"

She sighed and tried, without success, to get up. "Yeah, I'm here."

"Are you all right?"

"Just peachy."

Silence lasted long enough for her to feel guilty.

She scooted over a little on her butt to lean against the door. It was crazy but comforting to know he was just on the other side. "Shay?"

"Right here."

"I don't think I need any help getting up, but if I do…"

"As I said, I am here."

She exhaled sharply, then grabbed hold of the umbrella she'd used as a cane. After guiding the metal tip into a groove between the tiles, she tried to lift herself. The umbrella jumped the groove and slid on the tile until it collided with the toilet, making a loud clank.

Her heart jumped, and her hands started to shake.

"Olivia? I'm coming in."

She opened her mouth to tell him to wait, but he was beside her in a flash, scooping her up in his arms and cradling her to his chest. His heart was pounding as hard as hers.

"Are you all right?" he murmured into her hair.

"Embarrassed, but in one piece."

He gazed down at her, his anxious eyes roaming her face. "You should have waited for me."

Livy swallowed. His mouth was too close to allow her to think straight. "Well, you know, nature called and…"

She groaned, and briefly closed her eyes. *Nature called?* Oh, jeez. With any luck, maybe he didn't understand the term.

When she opened her eyes again, he was staring at her with such tenderness it made her breath catch. It meant nothing. He felt responsible for the accident. That's all.

"Are you ready for me to take you to bed?"

She almost choked at his phrasing. If he only knew how that sounded…

He did know.

The evidence was there, in the darkening of his eyes,

the slight flare of his nostrils. A thrill of excitement electrified her, made her head pound again.

She nodded and tried not to look at him. "Let me grab the umbrella."

He managed to snatch it up first, then carried her the short distance to the bedroom. It was the last one at the end of the hall, a small shoe-box-shaped room the Colemans used only when the other guest rooms were full.

Carefully he laid her down, his gaze briefly drawn to her thigh when the pink robe Rose had lent her fell open. Her stomach chose that moment to let out a loud, embarrassing growl.

He stepped back, one side of his mouth slowly lifting. "Are you trying to tell me something?"

"Ah, you have a sense of humor after all."

"I have an excellent sense of humor. And you have a very noisy stomach." His smile broadened when she glared at him. "I will get you something from the kitchen. What would you like?"

"Everyone's asleep by now."

"I am well aware of that fact."

"So, who's going to fix my grub?" She grinned at his puzzled frown, then yawned. "As much as I'd love to see you try to find your way around a kitchen, I'm too tired and achy to eat." She yawned again. "I need to rest up before Saturday."

He said nothing, only arched an eyebrow.

"Race day," she explained, and his eyes narrowed in disapproval. "I didn't ask for your opinion, and I don't want it."

She slipped under the covers and brought them up to her chin. The fabric was fine and soft, not like the raggedy edge of her worn hand-me-down quilt. She didn't belong here. Not in this room with the cheery floral wallpaper and expensive cherry furniture. Not even in this house. And certainly not with this man who wanted nothing more than a temporary distraction.

"My opinion is not the issue." He hooked a finger under her chin and brought her gaze up to meet his. Some unidentifiable emotion flared in his eyes. It almost looked like fear. "The doctor says you cannot ride. Promise me you will adhere to his orders."

She jerked away. Her head started to throb again. "I appreciate you bringing me back here and calling Doc and everything, but now you can just butt out."

Unexpectedly, he sat at the edge of her bed and touched her face. Slowly he angled her cheek away from him. "Did the doctor see this bruise?" he asked, tracing his finger near her right temple.

"I guess." It wasn't fair that he was making her so nervous her insides were hopping around like a bunch of Mexican jumping beans. She was too exhausted to put up a good defense. "Doc said I should get plenty of rest," she muttered. "And I can't do it with you practically sitting on top of me and poking around."

He cupped her cheek. "In my country, having rescued you means I am responsible for you."

"This is America, and no one's responsible for me but me." It wasn't easy to sound convincing when he was touching her like this. Or looking at her as if she were the only woman in the whole world. It made her breathing ragged, and her voice sound so thin.

"Why do you want to win this race? Is it only the money that interests you?"

She sank deeper into the soft pillow until contact was broken. "Mostly. But I do want everyone to see what a great horse Prince is. No one thought he was worth a darn when he was born.''

"There will be enough time for that later when you are well. Which brings us back to the money. If there is something you want, I can—''

"No. I know what you're going to say. And it's not that I don't appreciate it, but I've been on my own since I was sixteen and I've managed just fine.''

"I understand, but since money is not an issue for me—''

She smiled sadly. "Some things you just can't buy, Shay.''

He stiffened, a frown etching deep creases between his dark brows as he stared at her. "It was not my intention to insult you. I merely wished to help.''

"You didn't insult me.'' She tried to stifle a yawn with her fist. It didn't work. She could barely keep her eyes open any longer. "I probably didn't come across well. It's just that I've had enough charity in my life. I don't want to owe anyone anymore.''

He didn't say anything for a long time, and she was afraid she'd fall asleep before he finally did. Her eyelids were so heavy she could barely keep them lifted.

"I have a solution,'' he finally said. "You would be well cared for and owe me nothing. As my wife.''

Chapter Eleven

Livy had never had so many wild dreams in one night. Squinting at the morning sunlight streaming into the room through the blinds, she tried to remember one of them in particular. The one where Shay had asked her to be his wife. It was a crazy dream, and she was crazy for even trying to recall it. Good thing the events and images were too fuzzy. Otherwise they'd probably have her frazzled for the rest of the day.

Her watch lay on the nightstand, and she fumbled for it, already knowing it was way past time to get up. Not that she would be of much use today, but after someone picked up the crutches from Doc's office, she could do a few chores. Although Mickey would probably be hopping mad that he'd have the bulk of the mucking to do.

Before she could hobble out of bed, a knock at the door had her patting her hair down. She knew darn well what she looked like when she first awoke, and it wasn't pretty.

"Come in," she called, her voice already turning breathless in anticipation of seeing Shay.

The door opened slowly and Rose stuck her head inside. "Good morning." Using her shoulder to push the door open the rest of the way, she carried in a tray heaped with food and steaming coffee.

"Good morning back at ya." Livy glanced beyond Rose. No Shay. Disappointment nipped at her.

"He went to pick up your crutches and prescription." Rose set the tray down on the bed. "He should be back in a half hour or so."

Livy was glad Rose was too busy with the food to see how red her face had turned. Was her attraction to Shay that dang obvious? Apparently so.

"How are you feeling?" Rose glanced up from the tray. "You seem to have a little more color this morning."

Livy cleared her throat. "Yeah, I'm doing better. Thanks."

"Okay, I think we have everything." Rose stood back and studied the tray. "Coffee, orange juice, wheat toast with lots of butter, bacon. Ella says you don't like eggs."

"Gosh, Rose, you shouldn't have done all this. As soon as I have my crutches—"

"You will continue to rest," Rose finished. "Now, drink that orange juice."

Livy blinked. Normally she'd get steamed at someone ordering her around like that, but this time it gave her a warm, fuzzy feeling she didn't quite understand.

"Look, I haven't had anyone to mother in a long time." Rose smiled, picked up the orange juice and handed it to Livy. "Indulge me, okay?"

Livy accepted the glass, slightly shaken by the sudden realization that she liked being mothered by Rose. Other than Father Michael and a pair of part-time nurses who volunteered at the orphanage, no one had ever ministered to her this way. In fact, no one had, really. Not personally, anyway. Father Michael had treated all of his charges alike.

After gulping down half the juice, she set down the glass and gave Rose a shy smile. "You shouldn't be waiting on me."

"Your coffee is getting cold. So is the bacon." Rose grabbed the pillow beside Livy and plumped it up before slipping it behind her back. "There, you can get to the tray easier."

"You're making me feel really guilty."

"Why? You've been hurt. You need the rest and TLC."

"Yeah, but I'm liking it way too much."

Rose laughed. "Good. So am I."

The way she glowed, the happy tinkle of her laugh said she was telling the truth. Livy picked up a strip of the crisp bacon and nibbled it thoughtfully. How hard Rose's life must have been, not only because of the imprisonment, but being separated from her children, and yet she was always so cheerful. Shay didn't know how lucky he was, and Livy sure hoped he wised up soon.

Another knock sounded at the open door. Rose turned to see who it was, giving Livy an unobstructed view of King Zak.

He politely remained just outside the door. "How are you faring, Livy?"

"Come on in," Rose told him, then turned to Livy. "It's all right, isn't it?"

"Sure," Livy mumbled, floored that the king would come by to see her.

Even dressed in regular western-style clothing, he looked different than most men. He was tall and darkly handsome, and his clipped accent was very much like

Shay's. Rose had explained that the royal family had been educated in London, which made their English sound more British than American.

"You are feeling better?" He walked in and stood beside Rose.

"Much. Thank you," Livy said, and noticed how close together the two were. Closer than most acquaintances, or even friends would stand.

"Good. I do not want to disturb your breakfast. I understand Sharif has gone into town to pick up your medication. When he returns, we will all talk."

Talk? About what? Livy glanced at Rose, but her attention was centered on King Zak.

"I shall wait to have my meal with you," he said to Rose, then to Livy, "Rest well."

Neither woman said anything until he left the room, and then Rose said, "Oh, I almost forgot. A Father Michael called for you about fifteen minutes ago. Vi answered the phone and told him what had happened, and he said he'd stop by to see you this morning."

Livy groaned inwardly. Father Michael probably wanted to know when he could start getting the orphanage's roof fixed. He didn't know the money for the repair was to come from the race. Only that Livy was expecting a windfall.

She tentatively moved her ankle. It hurt like the devil. Still, she had time before the big day.

"You're looking a little pale again." Concern clouded Rose's eyes. "Should we have told Father Michael today wasn't a good time to drop by?"

"No, I was thinking about something else. Why don't you go eat with King Zak? I'm fine. Really."

"Then why aren't you eating your breakfast?"

Livy picked up a slice of toast, oozing with butter,

just the way she liked it, and took a small bite. She didn't really want it. Her stomach was so tied up in knots she wasn't sure she could keep any food down.

She'd opened her big mouth too soon, and now Father Michael and the kids were counting on her. She wouldn't let them down. No matter what it took.

Rose patted Livy's hand, bringing her out of her preoccupied silence. "Is this about you and my son?"

Livy shook her head. "I guess I'm still a little foggy is all."

"I'd be surprised if you weren't. Sharif should have waited and not pounced on you right after the accident. Men are so impatient sometimes."

Livy was even foggier than she thought. Rose was making no sense. Shay had been a perfect gentleman last night. Even when she'd wanted to bite his head off.

"If you decide you want to talk, I'm a good listener." She smiled. "After all, I do have some experience in this kind of thing. In the meantime, I'll leave you to eat your breakfast in peace and quiet."

Livy narrowed her gaze. "Talk about what?"

Another knock at the partially open door. It was Vi. She stuck her head in. "Hi. How are you doing?"

"Great." Livy immediately regretted the hint of sarcasm in her voice. Fortunately, she didn't think the other two women noticed.

"You have a visitor," Vi said. "May Father Michael come up?"

Livy groaned to herself. "Oh, why not?"

Vi and Rose exchanged glances, then Vi said, "I'll go get him."

Rose motioned to the tray of food. "Have some more before he gets here."

"Are you trying to fatten me up?"

"Certainly not." Rose laughed. "Especially not at this point. Just trying to get you better."

"What do you mean?"

Rose's eyes widened in surprise as she handed Livy the remaining orange juice. "Why would we want you to get well?"

"No. You said, not at this point."

A puzzled frown creased Rose's face as she studied Livy in speculative silence. "I think we need to talk."

Livy sighed and gingerly rubbed the bump on her head. She had definitely knocked it harder than she thought. Or else everyone had had too much hooch at the party last night. "Why does everybody suddenly want to talk to me?"

Mac stuck his head in the room. "Hey, you, don't you know how to ride a horse yet?"

"Very funny. Excuse me if I don't laugh. My head still hurts."

Mac's grin faded as he entered. "You okay, kid?"

"No, I've been abducted by aliens and sent to some parallel universe like on that TV show." Livy sank another degree under the covers. "Except I'm the only one acting normal."

"Aha. Must be a dream. You've never been—"

"Okay, that's enough," Rose cut in and made a shooing motion at Mac, who promptly started backing up. "Out. Livy needs to eat, then rest."

"Jeez, does everyone in the entire house know what happened?" Livy asked as soon as Mac left.

"Just the family. Except Jessica. She left to visit Abbie before we all got up."

Vi appeared at the door again. "You have a visitor."

She stepped aside and let Father Michael enter the room.

His normally sunny smile was clouded with sympathy, his blue eyes filled with concern, and Livy felt once again like the baby he had taken in all those years ago. He had been both father and mother to her, patiently answering her questions and explaining why it was important for her to eat her spinach.

She owed him so much.

"Morning, Father," she mumbled, still feeling like a kid. One who had done something incredibly stupid.

"Morning my foot. It's almost afternoon." He winked at Rose as he walked to the side of Livy's bed and pressed a palm to her forehead. Just like he always had when she was sick. "No fever. That's good."

"I'm not that kind of sick. Have you met Rose Coleman–El Jeved?"

"I've not had the pleasure." He gave Rose a big smile. "But I have heard about you."

Livy frowned, half listening to them exchange greetings. How had Father Michael heard of—

The newspaper!

Which meant he had seen the picture of her and Shay.

Livy wouldn't be surprised if she had a fever now. Her stomach rolled and her head grew light. Good thing she was already sitting down.

"So tell me what happened," Father Michael said, easing his slim frame onto the edge of the bed. His thinning red hair was a little too long as usual, and the wind had done a number on it. "A riding accident? That's awfully unlike you."

She stared blankly at him, unsure about mentioning Shay. Of course he was the one who'd rescued her, so there was no denying he was there. "I was exercising Prince down by the lake and he got spooked. I guess the trees blocked out too much of the moonlight and..." She shrugged.

"Well, no use crying over spilt milk, right?" He patted her hand. "You're both safe now."

She gave him a weak smile. "What did you call for, Father?"

He frowned, and a tapestry of fine lines fanned out from his eyes and mouth, making him look older than she remembered. "Oh, it's not important. We'll talk when you're well."

"Jeez, when I want to talk, no one else does," Livy muttered. "You know me better than that, Father. I'll go ape wondering what it was you wanted."

Rose cleared her throat. "I'll run down and get more coffee. How about I bring you up a cup, Father?"

"No, thank you. I'll not be staying much longer," Father Michael said, then remained silent until Rose left the room.

"Is it about the roof?" Livy spoke up first, both dreading the conversation and wanting to be done with it. She still didn't know what she was going to tell him.

"I really don't like discussing this while you're laid up."

"Hey, if I were you, I'd be glad to have my undivided attention."

He laughed. "Too true. You were an active child, all right."

Mildly put, to her mind. She bit her lip. Yet he'd always been there to pick up the pieces, to set her on her feet again. "Actually, I want to talk about the roof, too," she said slowly.

He must have sensed her hesitation, because alarm

flashed in his eyes, and then it was gone, replaced with a blank expression.

She just couldn't do it. How could she tell him she had to renege on getting the money to fix the roof because of her stupidity? Besides, she had a few days. Maybe she could still race. "Have you started getting estimates?" she asked brightly.

He seemed to relax. "As a matter of fact, we've found someone who can do it for a reasonable cost. A sum much better than I expected."

"Oh." She shifted, somewhat encouraged. She had savings left which she could get to in about a week. "How much?"

"Only eighteen thousand."

Livy swallowed hard. "Great." No way could she raise that much without first- or second-place prize money. Maybe her savings as a down payment, then part of her salary each month.

"The thing is, the contractor who gave us the bid has only a small window of time to do the work before his busy season starts. It's also based on a cash payment in full. I told him that wouldn't be a problem." He paused, frowning. "I know you said you'd have the money, but does this accident change things in any way?"

This was her opportunity to delay the repairs, to give herself time to find the money some other way. Her mind raced with possibilities.

"Olivia." Father Michael took her hand and sandwiched it between his two large callused ones. "I'm going to be totally honest with you. It's important you tell me where we stand, because if the roof doesn't get fixed, the board of health may have to close us down."

Her heart plummeted. "They can't do that! Where would all the kids go?"

"They can, and they should. I would be remiss myself if I didn't make other provisions for the children. It isn't safe. I've already had to relocate everyone from the west wing."

Livy shook her head in astonishment. "I didn't realize things were that bad."

"I'm not telling you this to burden you," he said gently, squeezing her hand. "I simply need to know where we stand."

"I'll have the money next week."

Relief slowly seeped into his expression. "You seemed unsure a minute ago."

She waved off his wariness. "I'm sorry, it must be because I'm feeling groggy."

"And here I am bothering you." He released her hand and stood. "I'll let you rest. Have you already placed your order for graham crackers and warm milk? Or shall I stop by with it later?"

Livy blinked, her mind still focused on the obstacle that lay ahead of her. And then she remembered. "You got me hooked on that. Every time I was sick, you told me dunking the crackers in the milk would cure me."

He winked. "It usually worked."

She grinned. "Yup, but only with the cinnamon kind."

He tousled her hair. "Get some rest." He stopped at the door. "Will you finally tell me where you're getting the money?"

Her smile briefly faltered. Good question. "Fat chance."

Father Michael shook his head, chuckling. "I always thought you'd outgrow that stubborn streak."

"I doubt we can look forward to that event." Shay appeared at the door with a set of crutches and a white pharmacy bag. "You are looking better today."

An amused smile curved the corners of his mouth as his gaze lingered on her, before it switched to Father Michael. He set the crutches against the wall and offered his hand. "I am Sharif Asad Al Farid, honored to meet you. I have heard admirable things about you and your work."

Shay obviously had a good, solid handshake, something in which Father Michael had always put enormous stock. Shay's silver tongue hadn't hurt matters, either. The transformation in Father Michael's face was startling. If Livy'd had any doubt he'd seen the newspaper photo, she didn't now. His reaction to Shay went from "you big jackass" to "what a nice young man."

She sighed loudly. "Gee, let me introduce you two."

Father Michael ignored her, and eyed the bag and crutches. "Thank you for taking care of Livy. I know what a handful she can be." He winked at her. "Just because you have crutches doesn't mean you should be hopping all over the place."

"That will not be a problem." Shay's gaze remained on her, hot and intense, making her forget to tell him to drop dead.

"I trust you're right." Father Michael sent her a skeptical look, then clapped Shay on the back as he passed him on his way out the door. "If you have time, stop by the orphanage. It would give the kids a thrill to meet real royalty."

Shay hesitated, looking somewhat startled. "I will arrange to do that."

"Good. Anytime."

Livy waited a minute for Father Michael to get down the hall and out of earshot before she said, "I don't want you going over there."

He seemed taken aback, his gaze narrowing in annoyance, and then curiosity. "You think I need your permission?"

"Okay, *please* don't go visit the orphanage."

He set the bag on the nightstand beside her and stood alarmingly close. "Why?"

"Because little girls are given enough hogwash—" at his puzzled frown, she amended "—lies about a Prince Charming or knight in shining armor coming to their rescue. They don't need those stupid fairy tales to come to life."

He grunted. "I came to your rescue."

"Yeah, but you're the cause of all my problems." And boy, were they doozies. She had to come up with the money for Father Michael, no matter what.

Shay looked genuinely surprised. "You are a very difficult woman to understand."

"Yeah, well, things were pretty simple before you showed up. Hand me my crutches, please."

He folded his arms across his chest and stared at her. "This is the way you treat me?"

Embarrassment washed over her. "Oh, sorry. Thanks for picking this stuff up for me." When he continued to glare, she asked, "What?"

"Olivia, you try my patience." He unfolded his arms and, with a sigh of exasperation, sat beside her at the edge of the bed. Close. Awfully familiar-like. "I like that you are so strong willed, and loathe it at the same time. I am sure the years will eventually even out both our temperaments."

"What in the heck are you talking about?" Instinct

made her want to cower beneath the covers. The heat of his gaze trapped her, drew her to him like a thirsty horse to water.

He brushed the bangs off her forehead and started to lower his face to hers. "As my future wife, of course."

Chapter Twelve

Livy stared at him in stunned disbelief, until she could feel the pressure of his lips against her forehead, and then she closed her eyes. Was this another crazy dream? Was she so stressed out she was having waking nightmares?

Not that marriage to him would be a nightmare. Or maybe it would. She didn't have a clue what was going on anymore.

He started to withdraw, and she opened her eyes, but he tipped her chin up and kissed her on the lips. Even with the feather-light kiss, her resolve began to melt, her heart started to pound, her head grew light.

When he pulled away, she almost protested.

"I know you are not feeling yourself," he said quietly. "Last night was hardly the optimum time to inform you of my decision. But in view of the media interest—"

"Back up."

At her piqued tone, he narrowed his gaze. "What has you so displeased?"

"Your decision?" She stiffened in indignation. "Your decision?" she repeated, words failing her as vague memories from last night clawed at her. "Are you proposing marriage?"

He blinked, sat a little straighter. "Well, yes, I suppose so."

"Or are you merely informing me of a foregone conclusion?" she asked. When he frowned in obvious confusion over the term, she added, "Let me put it another way. Are you crazy?"

Anger tightened his features. "I offer you my name and protection, and you call me insane?"

"Shay." She nearly shrieked his name and ended it with a groan of exasperation. "Number one, we don't know each other that well. Number two, you don't tell a girl you're going to marry her, you have to ask her."

"In Balahar—"

"I don't give a hoot about how things are done there, this is Texas." She paused to take a much-needed breath. "And...and there are certain ways of doing things so a girl will feel special at a time like this."

A tense silence stretched as he stared at her, his dark brows drawn together in bewilderment and aggravation. Possibly even a little regret. Or maybe that was more wishful thinking on her part. Assuming she was thinking at all. Which was definitely questionable considering she was sitting inches from Shay and discussing marriage, of all things.

She gave herself a mental shake. Obviously Shay felt responsible for her in some way, or maybe even his culture dictated he make the gesture. Still, the thrill of being asked to share his bed, not just for a night, but for a lifetime, was enough to jumble her thinking.

His face relaxed suddenly, and comprehension appeared to dawn. "Ah, you wish to have a ring. A ruby or a sapphire? Or perhaps the traditional diamond?"

She laughed, the sound ending on a whimper. "What's going on, Shay? You don't want to marry me."

Even though she knew that was the truth, the foolish child in her wanted him to deny it. She half held her breath waiting for the denial to leap into his eyes. But it didn't happen. His expression remained carefully noncommittal.

Since he didn't seem to be in a hurry to answer, she crawled over the covers to the foot of the bed and tried to reach the crutches.

He immediately got to his feet and blocked her efforts. Not that she was even close to snatching the crutches. She hated feeling this helpless, and her temper started to flare.

"Stop." He reached for her shoulders, but she jerked away.

Pain sliced through her ankle. Wincing, she crumpled into a heap in the middle of the bed. Her head started to throb again. She felt like having a good cry. But it hadn't done a bit of good the last time she'd had one, and she figured ten years hadn't changed much.

"Do you really find me that loathsome?" The thickness in Shay's voice forced her gaze to his.

To her amazement, his eyes were clouded with hurt. It had to be her imagination, except that he quickly looked away, arousing her suspicion further.

"You know better than that," she murmured, watching him, waiting for some clue to his thoughts. He didn't give an inch.

He ran a hand roughly through his hair, then paced to the window and stared outside in eerie silence.

She glanced at the crutches. Even if she could reach

them, she wouldn't be fast enough to stand up. Besides, where would she go?

Letting out a pent up breath, she tried to rein in her wild thoughts. It wasn't as if she were a prisoner. So why did she feel the need to run? Maybe because she didn't want to let go of the fantasy? Staying meant that at any minute the bubble would burst. Reality had a nasty way of doing that.

"Shay?"

He slowly turned to her, his lips pursed, his forehead creased in thought. He blinked, then took several long strides toward the door. She thought he was leaving, then jumped when he closed the door with a definitive click.

Her pulse had already started going nuts before he turned to her with a purposeful gleam in his eyes. He closed the distance between them in two seconds, and when she crawled back against the headboard, one side of his mouth lifted in a satisfied smile.

"My head hurts," she said, when he sat on the bed a mere inch away from her.

"How convenient." Uncertainty flickered in his face, and she felt only marginally bad about having lied.

"So does my ankle."

He opened the white pharmacy bag and removed a vial of pills, then filled a glass of water from the crystal carafe on the nightstand. "Here."

"What is it?"

"A painkiller prescribed by Dr. Simpson. It's the same thing he gave you last night."

"I don't want it." Her mood took a dive and she realized she was disappointed. She'd expected more than medication. "It makes me too sleepy."

"Perhaps more sleep would improve your disposition."

"I *like* being grouchy."

He tried to look stern, but a smile tugged at his mouth. "You do an admirable job."

"May I have my crutches now?"

"Why are you so anxious to run from me?"

Livy sighed. "It's not that...exactly. I have chores to do. I can't expect Mickey or any of the others to pick up all the slack."

A fierce frown drew his dark brows together. "You do not take my proposition seriously?"

"Marrying you?" Just saying the words sent a foolish shiver down her spine, her thoughts flying off in a hopeless direction. "Why? Do you love me?"

He reared back slightly in narrow-eyed suspicion. "I have a great fondness for you."

"Why?"

Annoyance flashed in his eyes. "Now I am not so sure."

She grinned in spite of herself.

"Your violet eyes. They intrigue me."

She lost the smile and made a face. "Great reason to get married."

"You will bear many brave, strong-willed children."

Livy blinked. "I thought you didn't want any. In fact, last night you said—"

"I am not a patient man, Olivia."

It wasn't her imagination that he moved closer, or that his eyes had darkened. "Is that supposed to win me over?"

The set of his jaw suggested she had pushed him too far. When he leaned toward her, she didn't retreat. Not because she wasn't afraid, but because it seemed almost impossible to move.

"Perhaps this will." He cupped her nape, drawing her closer, and covered her mouth with his.

The taste of sweet persuasion filled her, intoxicated her. His tongue tempted and taunted, then dove for surrender. The shy ineptness she should have felt didn't come. Nor did the fear that her inexperience would disappoint. She pushed toward him until his chest brushed her unbound breasts through the thin cotton nightshirt.

When one of his hands moved to her thigh, she nearly flinched, mostly in surprise. And then she realized he was insuring her ankle was not in harm's way, before he circled an arm around her waist and drew her so close she could barely breathe.

"Are you all right?" he whispered.

"I don't think so."

The breathlessness in her voice clearly told him her problem wasn't physical. He used the tip of his tongue to trace her jaw, then took a nip at the fleshy part of her ear. When he started to move down, she shamelessly arched her neck, exposing her throat.

It was the oddest sensation, to be mentally and physically urging him on as though her body had been taken over by an unseen spirit. Except she'd be a liar to deny she wanted him to touch her, that she didn't want this warm, squishy feeling to last and last. Maybe forever. Just as he had offered.

She shoved the dangerous thought aside. It wasn't hard. Thinking became nearly impossible when his mouth met her collarbone. And when he moved lower, wetting the thin cotton fabric, until he tongued her hardened nipple, she could barely remember her name.

Heat burst in the pit of her stomach, fanning lower, causing warm moisture to gather between her thighs. She didn't understand what was happening to her, but nor did she want it to end. Clutching Shay's shoulders tighter, she held her breath as he transferred his attention to her other breast.

When a knock sounded at the door, she almost didn't hear it. Probably wouldn't have, if Shay hadn't abruptly straightened. His eyes were glazed, his lips damp and tempting.

"Just a moment," he called out, his voice ragged and low. He pulled the covers up to her chest, his heated gaze lingering on the way her nipples puckered against the wet fabric, before he drew the quilt up to cover her.

He slowly stood, adjusting the fit of his slacks. She blinked at the bulge straining his fly, and her heart started a slow slam against the inside of her chest. When she tried to swallow, her mouth was so dry she could gather no saliva. More liquid heat pooled at her core.

He lifted her chin until their eyes met. His were so dark with desire that, to her horror, she had the strongest urge to force him back down again.

"We are not finished," he said, his voice still raspy, his breathing rough.

Incapable of forming a single coherent word, she silently watched him go to the door, then pause before opening it.

Mickey stood in the doorway, his hat in his hand, his goofy grin instantly disappearing when he saw Shay. Mickey's gaze shot questioningly to Livy. "I just stopped by to see how you were doing." He shifted from one scuffed-up booted foot to the other. "But I can come back later."

"Uh." Her voice wasn't working. She cleared her throat. "No, now is fine." She cleared it again. "Now that I have crutches, I'll be going back to the bunkhouse this afternoon, so I'll see you there."

Shay folded his arms across his chest and lifted a brow. Which meant he probably wasn't keen on her returning to the bunkhouse. Too bad.

She lowered her gaze to a sheen of moisture that remained on his bottom lip. Her nipples immediately hardened again at the reminder of where his mouth had been, and she clutched the quilt closer to her chest. Maybe she wasn't in such a hurry to go back to her own room after all.

Mickey twirled his hat in his hands and made a shuffling noise with his boots, drawing her attention. "Guess I'll see you later then."

"What?" She blinked. "Oh, yeah, later."

The curiosity in Mickey's face turned to suspicion, and he gave Shay a resentful look before leaving the room.

It was all her fault. She was such a quivering mass of nerves she could barely speak, and she had the attention span of a flea. Loosening her grip on the quilt, she sank against the headboard and sighed.

Shay closed and locked the door again and the tension sprang back, stiffening her spine, coiling inside her belly and making her mouth dry with anticipation.

"You see." He slowly headed toward the bed. Just watching, waiting, made her moist. "Yet another reason we should wed right away."

Embarrassment cooled her off. She stared at him, a

little dazed, wondering if he was referring to the strange things happening to her body.

He inclined his head toward the door. "I am sure he is not the only one speculating on our relationship."

Giddy relief bubbled in her chest. "You mean Mickey?"

Shay frowned as he stretched out beside her on the bed. As if it were the most natural thing in the world for him to do. As if he'd done it a hundred times before. Which he probably had...just not with her.

"You sound blasé," he said, eyeing her curiously. "I thought your reputation was of great concern to you."

"Of course it is. I just wasn't sure what you were talking about." Now that she knew, she pensively nibbled her lower lip. A crazy thought struck and her gaze flew to his. "So, you're willing to marry me just to save my reputation?"

He seemed surprised. "I would like to agree, especially if that would please you." He picked up her hand and kissed the back of it. "But that would not be accurate." Turning her palm over, he kissed the center, then found and held her gaze. "Of course I am delighted that marriage helps solve your problem, but I am not that altruistic."

Livy couldn't swear she knew for sure what that meant, but she was beginning to understand the look he was giving her. It sent a shiver from the back of her prickly neck straight down to the curl of her toes.

He let go of her hand and ran his palm up the side of her arm until he cupped her nape. As he drew her face closer to his, she dropped the quilt and felt the cooler room air against the damp fabric molded to her breasts.

Goose bumps surfaced her skin, and her entire body tightened. She needed little prodding to open her mouth to him, eager for his warm tongue to delve her secrets. Helplessly she pressed toward him, hoping he'd touch her breasts again.

Her horrendously lax reaction was beyond explanation. It was almost as if he were a powerful magnet and she was a mindless chunk of metal being pulled and sucked in his direction.

When his groan mixed with her sigh, and his hand tenderly spanned her jaw, she could almost convince herself that he did care for her, that love was his motivation. Of course he had to feel something. He couldn't kiss her this way and not, could he?

She hated being so woefully ignorant about men. Even though she worked with them all the time, when it came to intimacy or sex, she was at a total loss. Growing up with Father Michael as her guardian had left many unanswered questions about the subject. She hadn't known how much until her body started having all these strange reactions.

Shay slid his hand over her shoulder and down her arm. He pulled her closer still and placed her arms around his neck. The friction of his chest against her breasts felt so achingly sweet she thought she'd die from the sheer pleasure of it. Amazed at her own boldness, she pressed harder against him.

The impulsive move caused her body to shift and pain gripped her. She gasped. Shay immediately pulled away, his anxious eyes meeting hers before they drew to her ankle.

"Olivia." He gently took her by the shoulders and laid her back against the pillows. "I am so sorry. This is wrong."

It didn't feel wrong. In fact, his solid warm body engulfing hers felt frighteningly right. She didn't want him to stop. "It's okay," she said quickly, then bit her lip.

He didn't look smug, though, that she had essentially admitted she wanted his attention, only concerned.

She stared down at her hands, and noticed the bulge beneath his fly again. The knowledge eased some of her shyness and rekindled her excitement.

"Do you want the painkiller?"

She shook her head. "I'm okay now."

He touched her cheek. "There are other ways to pleasure you that do not require your active involvement."

At the low, gravelly tone of his voice, she swallowed. "I—I, uh, I'm not sure what you mean."

Surprise, then uncertainty showed on his face, and Livy was tempted to pull the covers over her head until he left the room.

"Olivia?"

His voice was gentle, almost sympathetic, but she looked away, too embarrassed to meet his eyes. With his fingers still on her cheek, he tried to guide her face back to his. When she wouldn't cooperate, he withdrew his touch.

Her entire body instantly protested, and she involuntarily moved toward him. The action was subtle, and she hoped he hadn't noticed and then all rational thought flew out of her head when he slipped the nightshirt off her shoulder and found her bare breast.

She whimpered and strained forward, clutching his upper arm.

"Shh." He urged her to lie back down. "Relax."

"What are you doing?" Her breath caught when he lightly pinched her nipple. "Shay?"

"Showing you how good we are together," he murmured, pushing the fabric aside and touching her nipple with the tip of his tongue, before sucking it into his mouth.

She pressed herself into the mattress and closed her eyes, gripping the sheets for support. Heat pulsed throughout her body, hitting harder one place in particular.

Marriage suddenly didn't sound so out of the question. If he could make her feel like this, something had to be right. There had to be some kind of connection between them.

He moved his mouth to her other breast and, in the second it took, she thought she'd go out of her mind in anticipation. She reflexively moved a hand to his shoulder, and he manacled her wrist with his strong fingers, keeping her arm pinned to her side.

He released her breast, his tongue trailing it as he pulled away, then looked at her, his eyes glazed and dark. "Stay still. Let me love you."

Livy held her breath. Love? What did he mean? Her thoughts were starting to get awfully jumbled, totally irrational. It would be easy if she did believe he loved her. Marriage to him would solve some of her problems. Her reputation would no longer be an issue, and the orphanage would undoubtedly get more than a new roof.

God help her, but above all, the thought of waking up beside him each morning held more appeal by the second. It wasn't only the delicious things he was doing to her body, but the hungry yet tender look on his face that was melting her faster than an ice cube in July.

"There's something you should know," she whispered, barely recognizing her own voice.

He slid his hand up her thigh and gently parted her legs. Panic seized her and she clamped them shut again. He didn't react, only rested his palm at the juncture of her thighs and leaned down to kiss her on the lips.

"I'm trying to tell you something—"

His mouth covered hers, silencing her, making her thoughts scatter. When he parted her legs again, she didn't stop him. When his hand moved back up to cup her mound, she still didn't stop him. And when his fingers slid into her liquid heat, she nearly fell apart.

"Oh, ah...ah." She whimpered and reflexively shifted her hips. His fingers went deeper. "Shay." She covered her mouth with a fist to keep from moaning too loudly.

"You are so hot and wet," he whispered close to her ear, then slid his tongue along the shell before nipping at her earlobe. He murmured something in another language, his breathing so rough it pelted her neck with little warm puffs.

When he suddenly hesitated, his hand withdrawing slightly, she pushed her hips up to resume contact. He mumbled something again, groaning so that she couldn't even tell if it was English.

Her entire body felt as though it were on fire, that it could erupt at any second. Her skin prickled and tightened and when he plunged his fingers in one more time, she almost flew off the bed. She closed her eyes, warmth invading her every pore, an unfamiliar sensation building and building, the momentum robbing her of breath and reason.

The explosion came. Reds and oranges flashed behind her lowered eyelids. Heat pulsed through her veins, warming her skin, bringing a flush to her entire body. Tears filled her eyes, seeping from the corners, spilling down to her hair. Her heart pounded so hard, it would surely beat through her chest.

She nearly cried out, but Shay's mouth was on hers, his tongue replaying the action of his fingers. She clutched his shoulder, looking for balance, for the room to stop spinning, and he reluctantly pulled back.

Heaven help her, but she hadn't meant to stop him. What could she say now? Did she have the guts to draw him back?

He angled away and gazed solemnly at her, his eyes still glassy. "You are a virgin."

Livy nodded. "I tried to tell you."

His mouth lifted in a slow, satisfied smile. "You will make a fine first wife."

Chapter Thirteen

A freezing wet blanket couldn't have sobered her more quickly. She pushed his hand away and tried to sit up. Maybe she'd heard wrong. Maybe he was joking. "First wife?"

Shay blinked, looking slightly unfocused. Running a hand through his hair, he straightened and met her eyes. "Yes."

"You're already planning our divorce?" She tried to laugh but ended up sounding pathetic.

He frowned. "Of course not. You will always remain my wife. No matter how many others I marry."

Stunned, she opened her mouth, but nothing came out. He looked serious.

"Being chosen first is an honor you will forever hold."

"You jerk! You—" She shook her head, shame and hurt blocking her air passages, jumbling her thoughts.

"Olivia, what are you doing?" He reached for her when she crawled across the bed, but she dodged him, even though her ankle hurt like the dickens.

"Don't touch me. Just—" She put up a warning hand. "Just don't." She stretched to reach for the crutches and almost fell flat on her face. But she managed to snag one of them and they both tumbled toward her.

There was no easy or graceful way to position herself in order to maneuver the crutches under her arms. Her nightshirt rode up her thighs, but she didn't care. She just wanted to get out of the room as quickly as possible. Besides, how much more could she humiliate herself? The way she'd let him touch her...

Anger pricked her and she nearly lost control of the crutches. Her ankle hurt like hell, and so did her ego. First wife? Humiliation washed over her again. How could she be so damn gullible? How could she have thought she was special to him? He could have any woman he wanted.

"Olivia, please." Shay moved between her and the door. "I understand I have upset you. I should have explained how our culture allows—"

"I don't give a damn about your culture. Move out of the way."

"Olivia." He put out a hand to her.

"Move."

Their gazes locked for a moment and then she looked away, not wanting him to see how much he'd hurt her. Something in her eyes must have warned him to back off, because he opened the door for her and stepped aside.

She hobbled out, the crutches still unfamiliar as she plodded down the hall. It was going to be a real trick navigating the stairs, but she'd slide down the banister if she had to, anything to get away from him.

Shay watched her slowly make her way down the hall. There was no way she was going to be able to safely descend the staircase. But he knew his assistance would not be welcomed. He hoped she had enough sense to wait for someone else's help.

He had no choice. He hurried to the opposite suite of rooms and knocked on his father's door without much hope he would still be there. To his surprise, King Zak opened the door. Behind him, Sharif saw Rose sitting on a chair near the window.

A flurry of emotion momentarily distracted him and he stared blankly at his father. What was Rose doing here? What were *they* doing?

"Sharif? You wanted something?"

He blinked. "I need your help. Olivia is trying to go down the stairs by herself. I am afraid she will be further injured."

Rose jumped to her feet.

His father scowled at him as he pushed through the door. "Why would you let her attempt such a thing?"

Fortunately, his father did not wait for an answer but hurried down the hall after Olivia. Rose started to follow him but paused, frowning. "What happened between you two?"

He stiffened. "Apparently, she does not wish to become my wife."

Her gaze narrowed. "That's all?"

Sharif's laugh was without humor. "How can you ask that? When my father made you a queen, did you not consider that an honor?"

"Is that what you did, Sharif, ask Livy to be your queen?"

He glared at her a moment, but she did not cower or look the least contrite. "Olivia needs your help," he said before he turned around and headed for his own room.

Anger and resentment ate at him. Was he not trying

to do the right thing by marrying her? As his wife she would lead a life of luxury, she would be denied nothing. She could have many horses finer than Prince.

He slammed the door to his room and eyed the unpacked suitcases his attendant had placed in the corner. There was no reason for him to stay any longer. He had met Rose and his brothers. They were his family and he would welcome seeing them again in the future. But not here in Texas. Not where he would see Olivia again.

Reluctantly he moved to the window and pushed aside the burgundy-and-gray drapes. If Olivia was on her way to the bunkhouse he would be able to get a glimpse of her. Better to see her from afar, where her wounded violet eyes could not haunt him.

He had hurt her and he knew exactly how and why. The knowledge helped little. He was a damn coward. Fear had motivated him to devalue his proposal. She was making him feel weaknesses he did not want to face. Marriage and commitment had never preoccupied his mind as they had in the past few days.

The entire idea was absurd. Especially with someone like Olivia, a woman who could not be more unsuitable. She was not only a commoner, but a laborer as well. She knew nothing of the social graces. Her attire was inappropriate. She lacked the experience to please a man.

Slowly he exhaled, hoping to loosen the building tension in his belly, and stretched his neck from side to side.

He could still taste her. And her scent clung to him like wet sand on his heated skin. Even his dreams last night had been filled with violet eyes and a soft pink mouth. A face that housed an old soul, one who had been dealt more in one life than three should suffer. Yet what he remembered most was her smile, full of hope and excitement. Her past did not rule her.

Sharif sighed with disgust. Although it was true that his country's laws and custom allowed him to take more than one wife, he had never considered doing so. Just as King Zak had not, nor had his father before him. Western influence had altered the tradition decades ago.

Giving up on the notion he would see her, he turned from the window just as the knock sounded at his door. He was tempted to ignore it, assuming it was either Rose or his father. But along with their recriminations could possibly be news of Olivia. All he wanted to know was that she had returned safely to her room.

He opened the door. King Zak and Rose stood side by side, a disappointed look on her face, a hint of curiosity in his father's. Sharif said nothing, but merely turned around and headed for the tray of brandy, knowing they would follow him.

"It is not yet noon." His father eyed the snifter Sharif filled with the amber liquid in blatant disapproval.

"Want one?" Sharif took a hearty sip.

"Yes, I'll have one," Rose said, and both men looked at her in surprise. "Drowning my sorrow sounds like a good idea. I finally meet my youngest son and I find out he's a jackass."

Sharif nearly choked. Even his father's eyebrows shot up at Rose, his expression bewildered, perhaps displeased at seeing this side of her.

It was almost a shame, Sharif thought. He was beginning to like the woman, but he knew his father would not tolerate such insolence.

After an awkward pause, King Zak cleared his

throat. "Your mother is right. You have been behaving like a bit of a jackass these past few days."

Hurt that his father took Rose's side, Sharif sent him a resentful look, then took his brandy with him to the window and shoved the drapes aside. Two boarders were headed toward the stables. But no sign of Olivia. "Did someone help her to the bunkhouse?"

"Do you really care?" Rose asked, and Sharif refused to turn around. "Alex took her."

Silence festered.

Sharif took a sip he no longer wanted. "She should not be left alone."

"I apologize. I haven't been fair," Rose said sweetly, and out of the corner of his eye, he watched her take a chair near the window and curl her legs beneath her. "I'd love to hear your side of the story."

Sharif swallowed hard at the unappetizing thought. And then shame rolled into anger. He owed Rose nothing. She was purposely trying to provoke him.

"Yes," his father agreed as he sat beside Rose. "I too would like to hear you out."

Sharif clenched his jaw and stared at the traitors. "I offered her my name, my protection. Is that not an honor?"

"Okay," Rose said slowly, "let's say she accepted your proposal but said she was going to continue seeing Mickey on the side. But of course you would always remain number one. Would you consider that an honor?"

Mickey? The other hand? Sharif reared back his head in stunned outrage. "She is involved with that— with that—"

"Careful," Rose warned. "I was merely being hypothetical, but I am glad to see you have a streak of jealousy concerning Livy.''

Denial sprang to his lips. But he quickly discarded it as unimportant. ''That analysis is seriously lacking. My proposal descends from a tradition rich in—''

His father cut him off with a loud sound of exasperation. ''Sharif, enough. We both know better. The old ways died long ago.'' King Zak's probing black eyes narrowed suddenly. ''You are afraid.''

''Afraid?'' Sharif reacted with a short bark of laughter. ''Nonsense.'' He left the window and returned his glass to the tray. He had no intention of sticking around and listening to foolish speculation.

''Ah, I see I have uncovered a truth.''

Anger tempted Sharif's tongue, but he used all his reserve to curb the impulse to strike back. ''You may speculate as you wish. I have things to do.''

''Wait.'' His father held up a hand. Sunlight caught the large ruby ring he wore and threw a muted red glow across the wall. ''This is not the time to walk away. You have hurt that young lady, my son, and all your denial will not convince me you do not care for her.''

Sharif stared at the spot where the red glow had tinted the wall an otherworldly sheen. The brilliance was gone now, leaving a plain cream stucco finish, but he could not seem to drag his gaze away from it.

It was not possible that he could have feelings for Olivia in such a short time. He had dated many women far more compatible and suitable, but he had never entertained the thought of marriage. Yet no matter how he tried to rationalize his overwhelming confusion, what his father said was the truth. He did care for Olivia. But he had let his pride overrule his good sense.

''I only knew Ibrahim for a week before I agreed to

marry him,'' Rose said softly, as if she could read his thoughts. ''There was no question in my mind that we were meant to be together. I still miss him.''

Sharif looked at her, amazingly serene with her intrusion into his thoughts. It was comforting somehow, to have that bond with her, and not unnerving as he may have expected.

''Look into your heart, Sharif.'' His father's face had softened. ''There is a reason you asked this woman to marry you. Perhaps your heart accepts what your mind cannot.''

He briefly closed his eyes. Had he been the one who had fallen and hit his head? And not Olivia. Was this all a dream? None of the events of the past twelve hours made sense. Not even his proposal. His father had certainly never urged him toward marriage before. Queen Nadirah had been the one who was of the opinion that a good union would tame his wild ways. But King Zak had always kept his counsel on the subject.

Although Sharif had never truly considered a harem, the idea of committing to one woman for the rest of his life was almost inconceivable. Would he not be bored? Would the responsibility of a family not grow too confining?

His thoughts drew back to Olivia and her wide violet eyes, her infectious smile that made everything seem a little more bearable. Her big heart and wise words had shed a different light on his relationship with Rose. Olivia had given him the gift of gratitude. And he had rewarded her with pain.

He shook his head, realizing the true irony of his miserable situation. The thought of not being with Olivia was equally inconceivable. Still, marriage was so final. Surely they could come to some sort of agreement.

"I have to go talk to her," he said finally, and met Rose's eyes. They were kind and reassuring, and he was jolted with another realization. He liked her. She had not judged or coddled him. Without a doubt she would not always agree with him. But in her expressive blue eyes, there was no question she would always be on his side.

Impulsively he went to her and picked up her hand. She flinched a little, a startled look flickering across her face.

"Thank you." He bowed his head and kissed the soft skin above her knuckles. "Mother."

The word still felt strange on his tongue, and a sting of disloyalty gave him a moment's pause. But he knew the woman who had raised him, the woman who would always be the mother of his heart, would have been equally touched by the mist brightening Rose's eyes. Queen Nadirah would have wanted him to honor the woman who had given him life. Selfishly he had used her memory to create a distance between him and Rose.

Total acceptance would come gradually, he knew, but he was willing to make a start. And Rose, fully composed like the queen she was, smiled graciously, knowingly, then she too gave a slight bow. "You're very welcome."

He swallowed hard and thought about heading straight out the door without another word. Instead, he turned to his father. A man known for his stoicism, it was no surprise that King Zak's expression revealed little. Except Sharif saw the gleam of approval and pride in his coal-black eyes.

"Tell me, Father, why become involved in this matter? You have never even hinted at marriage, and you barely know Olivia.''

''True. But one thing I do know. In the past few days, you have finally become a man.''

LIVY RARELY CURSED. At least not like the rest of the hands did, but every time she tried to mount Prince, she let a string of words fly that would have made Father Michael faint.

She leaned against the stall door, relying heavily on her crutches, beads of perspiration forming above her upper lip and eyebrows. Her head hurt like the devil, and her ankle felt as if it was on fire.

Prince shook his head, whinnying, his liquid brown eyes full of confusion. When he tried to nuzzle her, she did her best to reassure him without falling on her fanny.

''It's not you, boy. I promise.'' She gingerly lifted her hand, careful to keep the crutch secure under her arm, and stroked his neck. ''We still have three more days, though. By then my ankle will be as good as new and we're going to show them you're the best and fast-est horse in three counties.''

She didn't believe a word she'd said. Except for Prince being the best and fastest horse. He was. But she had a horrible feeling she wasn't going to be the one to prove it.

Looking down at her discolored, swollen ankle made her sick. How could this happen now? Right before the race. Her chest tightened with defeat. If there was any way humanly possible, she would have made it into the saddle by now.

Of course she could ask Mickey to help her. He was about the only one she might be able to badger into it.

And then again, maybe not. He was a good friend and all he had to do was take one look at her ankle and he'd know she was asking for trouble. Maybe more than she could handle.

She took a deep breath, straightened, then positioned the crutch to act as her left leg. Before she could even begin to raise her right foot, the left crutch wobbled and she lost her grip. The crutch fell forward, spooking Prince. Livy leaned back in the nick of time. She narrowly missed being bumped by Prince, but unable to keep her balance, she landed hard on the stall floor.

Tears of pain stung her eyes. Helpless anger surged through her, and she pounded the ground with her fist. She had no choice. She had to ask for Mickey's help. Maybe if she explained about Father Michael and the roof for the orphanage she could talk Mickey into it.

And then what? How was she going to keep her foot in the stirrup?

She scooted back until she was safely away from Prince's restless hooves and slumped against the wall. It wasn't in her nature to give up so easily, but the truth was, she wasn't even sure how she was going to get back up.

Damn that Shay. This was all his fault.

First wife.

Humiliation overrode the throbbing in her ankle. And then she remembered how his mouth had felt on her breasts, on her lips, how she had grown so hot and moist and wonderfully feminine that she thought the earth had risen to meet heaven.

Worst of all, she'd felt loved. And that was her fault. She should have known better than to think a man like him would be seriously attracted to her. What did she have to offer him? Why would he want her? Her own parents hadn't.

Livy closed her eyes and bumped the back of her head twice against the wall. That useless thought made her angriest of all. She didn't really feel unwanted or discarded just because her parents hadn't had the resources to keep her. Other kids at the orphanage felt abandoned, unlovable. But she'd always tried to not take it personally. Father Michael had taught her that.

And now she was going to have to disappoint him. More depressing, she'd have to stand by and watch the orphanage close.

No way. She couldn't do it. Father Michael had devoted his entire life to helping kids at St. Mary's. Where would he go?

She pushed back hard against the wall and tried to inch her way up. Splintered wood dug through her shirt and into her skin. Perspiration dampened her neck and arms from her efforts, and still she couldn't get up.

"I knew I would find you here."

At Shay's caustic voice, Livy gritted her teeth and looked up. The anger she expected to see was absent. Fear darkened his eyes as his gaze flicked over her, slowly, as though examining her, making sure she was okay. Her own annoyance lessened. But not totally.

"So, now that you have, get lost."

"Do you need help getting up?"

His tone was so darn patronizing she really wanted to ignore him. She disliked admitting that she did need help, but she didn't want to spend the night in the stall, either. And then again, he'd probably have to touch her...

"When I'm ready, I can get up just fine." She folded her arms across her chest and pretended to be completely relaxed. "Why don't you go start looking for engagement rings? There's a Costco two counties over. You can probably get rings and wedding invitations in bulk."

He flinched slightly, which didn't make her feel a bit better. She sorely wished she hadn't even brought up the subject. Now he probably thought she was still smarting over it. A lump formed in her throat and she had a mighty time trying to swallow around it.

"Olivia." He started to shake his head, and she knew she didn't want to hear what he was going to say. "I am truly sorry for—"

"Stop." Without thinking, she tried to get up, then sank back against the wall when a sharp pain knifed her ankle. "You don't need to say anything." Her voice sounded unnatural, breathless from the pain. She lifted her chin and silently cleared her throat. "I knew you weren't serious."

He stared at her, disbelief all over his face before his expression went blank. "Of course." Indecision briefly flickered in his eyes. "I would like to help you to your room. Surely there is nothing you can do here."

If he'd noticed the saddle she had hoodwinked one of the part-time hands into putting on Prince, he ignored it. He picked up the fallen crutch, then extended a hand to her.

"I told you I can get up on my own just fine." She stubbornly refolded her arms across her chest. "And if you don't mind, I'd like to be alone with Prince."

"I mind," he said, and bent down and scooped her up before she knew what was happening.

Being cradled in his arms and pressed against his chest as she was, all the memories of their intimacy came rushing at her like torrents of early summer rain.

Surprisingly, she felt no embarrassment, only the same sultry, sensual contentment she'd experienced earlier. As if everything was right in the world.

But it wasn't. Not even close. Her ankle wasn't going to heal in time for the race, and the orphanage wasn't going to get a new roof and would probably have to close. And she didn't think she could do a damn thing about it.

"What are you thinking?" he whispered, his mouth close to her ear, his warm breath stirring the hair on her neck.

She sniffed. "I think I hate you."

Chapter Fourteen

She was tired, medicated, Sharif decided, and not thinking clearly. At least he hoped that was the problem. He still was unsure as to how he felt about her. All he knew for certain was that he could not bear to see her hurt anymore. He would make sure that no one helped her attend the race, or they would pay dearly.

He had noticed the saddle on Prince, something she could not have accomplished by herself. She would not mount it, though, even if he had to guard her twenty-four hours a day.

Oddly, the thought was far from unpleasant. He almost wished for her defiance. Anything that would give him a reason to assume her guardianship.

"Hate me if you will," he finally said, and tightened his arms around her. "But you must obey the doctor's orders and that means returning to the main house."

"Screw you. Need that translated?"

He fought a smile. "I assumed you were no longer interested."

She squinted at him. "I'm sure you have other things to do besides harass me, so if you'll just set me down..."

"As soon as we get you to your room."

She sighed. "I guess I don't have much choice. If that's what it takes to get rid of—" She twisted to turn around, and he almost lost his grip. "Hey, you're passing the bunkhouse."

"Yes, we are."

"You can't make me do this, damn it." She pounded a fist into his arm, and when he held her closer she tried to jerk her body free.

"All right. Be still." The blow landed on muscle and he barely felt it, but he worried that she could reinjure herself, so he gently put her down.

She stood on one foot until he correctly positioned the crutches in front of her. After he was sure she had control of one of them, he let it go and grasped her waist until she could steady herself. She uttered not a single protest, and he could see the strain of her efforts tensing her face. Moisture gleamed on the skin above her upper lip, and tendrils of hair clung to her damp cheeks. What she needed was some bed rest, and if it meant he had to back off, he would do it. For now...

"Thanks for your help." Her tone was crisp, impersonal, and she turned and headed back toward the bunkhouse.

He waited for a few minutes, to make sure she did not return to the stables. When she disappeared into the bunkhouse without once looking back, he walked the short distance to the stables himself. Prince's tack needed to be removed, and although Sharif had no doubt Olivia would ask someone to tend to the horse, he had the sudden urge to tackle the chore.

Having seen the staff at the palace do it hundreds of times, he was fairly certain he could remove the saddle. Unlike preparing a horse to ride, if he messed up, no one would get hurt. Prince may be a little unhappy, but a few cubes of sugar would restore his spirits.

By the time Sharif got to Prince's stall, the horse was already snorting with impatience. But he settled down as soon as Sharif approached him, and Sharif easily ran the stirrups back up as far as the stirrup bar. He undid the girth on the right side and carefully placed it over the saddle. As he had seen his attendant do, he held the saddle and the numnah together while he lifted the saddle off Prince.

It seemed so easy he felt foolish for doubting himself. But Alex's remark about learning to do things for himself had struck a raw nerve. Sharif really had no practical skills. Of course, until now, he had had little use for any. His wishes were always carried out to his satisfaction.

Maybe that was the attraction to Olivia. She seemed so disinterested in his title, or his wealth, or in him for that matter. He remembered how she had responded earlier this morning, and he smiled. On second thought, her interest in him was not totally lacking.

He sobered suddenly and leaned heavily against the wall, the weight of his unexpected realization almost too much for him to bear. Olivia's only interest was in him, the man. Not his possessions or power. Not the palace in which he lived, nor the fast cars he drove. She cared about none of those things. She cared only that he was an honorable man, a good son, and someday perhaps, that he would be a good father.

And damn, but he wanted to be all of those things.

LIVY GAVE IN and reached for the vial of painkillers. Not only had she been stupid enough to try to ride too soon, but she'd hurt her ankle again. She'd tried to wait

out the throbbing, but it hadn't subsided in the hour
since she'd crawled into her own bed. And she needed
a clear head.

It was obvious she wasn't going to be able to make
the race. It was equally obvious that she was the only
hope for the orphanage's new roof. The one thing not
obvious was what she could do about it.

Lying in bed and staring at the ceiling, she reviewed
her options. She could explain to Father Michael and
he would immediately let her off the hook without a
single word of reproach. But the orphanage would still
need the roof.

Or she could go to the Colemans.

No, she couldn't. They'd contributed so much to the
orphanage already. This was her problem. She'd never
relied on anyone for help before, and she had no intention of doing it now. Besides, she did have another
resource.

She took a deep, painful breath, the thought of what
she'd have to do staggering. But did she have a choice?

Before she lost her nerve, she swung her legs out of
bed, then reached for her crutches. The painkiller
hadn't started working yet and her ankle hadn't quit
throbbing, but if she didn't get to the phone now, she'd
likely crawl under the covers and let the rest of the day
slip away.

Balancing on the crutches, she opened her bedroom
door. Shay stood out in the hall, less than a foot away,
his fisted hand lifted and ready to knock.

The surprise of seeing him nearly sent her tumbling
backward, but she steadied herself and glared at him
when it looked as though he was about to touch her.
"What do you want?"

He stared back in narrow-eyed suspicion. "Where are you going?"

"Square dancing."

He snorted. "If you were at the main house, you would have someone to bring you anything you needed."

"You mean, someone could pee for me, too?"

He gave her an annoyingly patronizing look. "I will wait for you here."

"Don't you rich people ever have *anything* to do?"

He folded his arms across his chest. "Unless you prefer that I escort you."

"Never mind." She hobbled back a step and shut the door.

The look of surprise on his face just as the door closed was almost enough to boost her spirits. But the fact was, he'd just made her delay the unpleasant task of calling Cord Brannigan.

OLIVIA WAS UP TO SOMETHING. Of that, Sharif had little doubt as he roamed the common living area of the bunkhouse, looking for something to read, or anything that would occupy his time and attention.

The other hands were all outside working and unavailable. Perhaps Olivia only meant to go to the kitchen for something to eat, or she really did have to go to the rest room. Surely she did not intend to try to mount Prince again. The idea was so clearly futile. But then why had she looked so guilty coming out of her room?

He found an old equestrian magazine and settled on a lumpy brown plaid couch with it. He had no idea what he hoped to accomplish by staying, except that, if Olivia needed anything, he would be here to assist her. There was also that small seed of doubt that she would follow the doctor's orders and stay off her feet.

A click sounded from down the hall, the slow opening of a door perhaps, and he set the magazine down and remained perfectly still. A moment later, he heard the thump of her crutches on the wooden floor.

He stayed quiet, waiting to see where she was going, but the thumping stopped abruptly. After waiting another minute, guilt started to eat at him. Eavesdropping and spying were not habits he endorsed. He was about to call out and make known his presence when he heard her voice.

Certain no one else was in the house, he frowned. And then he realized she was on the phone. He got up, undecided whether he should step outside or simply let her know he was present. Although what he truly wanted to do was secretly listen and make sure she was not making arrangements to foolishly enter the race.

When he overheard Prince's name and a dollar sum, his gentlemanly instincts flew out the window and he moved closer to hear better. Was she paying someone to ride in her place? Or paying them to help her into the saddle?

The floor creaked beneath his shoes, and her voice died. After a few moments, she mumbled something, then quickly hung up the phone. The thump of her crutches echoed down the hall, and again he heard the click of her door.

He thought briefly about confronting her but figured it would do little good. What he really needed was a plan that would keep her safe until the race was over. And he had a good idea what he needed to do.

LIVY WAS STARTING to get pretty good with her crutches. Which produced dangerous thoughts, and she had to remind herself that being able to get around on her crutches didn't mean her ankle was getting any better. At least not good enough to climb into a saddle.

If there was any way possible she'd do it, and worry about her ankle later. But she also had the risk of injury to Prince to consider.

The thought of him, and what she was about to do was so overwhelming that she had to hurry toward the stables before she burst out crying and crumpled into a heap in front of the bunkhouse. Not a good way to keep her affairs private. Of course, around here, it wouldn't take long for everyone and their dog to know what she'd done.

Forcing her thoughts away from Prince, she concentrated on coordinating her steps with the crutches, on the crispness of the air, the blue of the sky. It didn't seem fair that it should be such a beautiful day. Not when her heart felt so heavy she thought it might sink to her toes. As soon as she entered the stables and heard Prince's familiar neigh, her eyes filled with hot tears.

She quickly blinked them away, then stopped to wipe her face with her shoulder when a couple fell on her cheek. How was she going to face each day without giving him his sugar, or having him nuzzle her neck?

If she didn't get the money for the orphanage, she couldn't face another day, period.

She swallowed hard and started toward Prince's stall again when she heard voices. Low murmuring, really. And then a sob.

She froze, and listened hard. Randy Coleman's voice rose a little from about three stalls down. Livy couldn't identify the other person's whispers, except that she knew it belonged to a woman, and she ducked into an empty stall, not sure what to do. If the woman was that boarder, Savannah, Livy would just die of embarrassment. She'd also be horribly disappointed in Randy.

Although it was hard to believe he'd do anything to hurt Vi. Livy had always thought that if she ever got married, she'd want a relationship just like the Colemans. They seemed to be the perfect loving couple, and yet, Randy had acted awfully strangely in the past few weeks.

After a couple of minutes of silence, Livy decided it was safe to leave the stall when she heard Randy's voice again, closer this time.

"Wait, don't leave." The woman sniffed, and he added, "Okay, I'll tell you what's going on. It was supposed to be a surprise, but I can't see you staying all worked up like you've been."

"What kind of surprise?"

Recognizing Vi's voice, broken as it was, Livy breathed a soft sigh of relief.

"For your birthday," Randy said. "I'm throwing you a big party."

"My birthday? But...but I'm going to be fifty!" Vi started sniffling again.

"Oh, honey, are you upset over that?" Randy's tone softened. "But you keep getting more and more beautiful every year. The other women in this county ought to be upset. Not you."

Livy clamped a hand over her mouth when she almost sighed out loud.

Vi half laughed, half sobbed. "But you've been spending so much time with Savannah...and she's so pretty. And *young*. Most of my jeans are older than she is."

Randy reacted with a short bark of laughter. "She's also a party planner."

"A what?"

"I can't believe you thought anything was going on between her and me. Oh, Vi, you know me better than that."

Vi's muffled sniffles subsided. "I'm getting your shirt all wet."

"You don't hear me complaining," Randy said, and Livy could almost hear his smile, see the twinkle in his eyes as he gazed lovingly at Vi.

"Are you really planning a party for me?"

"Yup, you and Jessica, and I'm inviting the whole damn county."

"Great. Now, everyone will know I'm over the hill. Let's just have the party for Jess. Turning twenty-five is quite a milestone."

"Nice try." Randy planted a noisy kiss somewhere that made Vi giggle. "But I want to honor both my favorite girls."

"Does Jess know about this?"

"Are you kidding? She's been too busy fighting with Nick to notice anything. Hey, how about a roll in the hay before we head back?"

"Randy…" Vi drawled in warning, laughing at the same time, and Livy felt like crawling into a hole for eavesdropping. "Do you think we should be worried about Jessica and Nick?"

"About them bickering? I think we should be more concerned about having to pay for a wedding soon."

"Oh, Randy. I'm serious. I sure wish they'd get along better. In fact, I wouldn't mind having him as a son-in-law at all."

They were suddenly right on the other side of the

stall, and Livy stayed totally still until their voices got
farther away, then she slowly poked her head out and
watched them head arm in arm toward the main house.

She'd felt so darn guilty hearing their private conversation, but she'd had no idea that they were discussing something so personal when she'd ducked out
of sight. And she wasn't ready to explain to anyone
why she was selling Prince. She could barely hold on
to the thought herself. Even picturing Father Michael
standing out in the cold rain surrounded by his charges
didn't have the same impact it had an hour ago when
she'd purposely created the image to keep from crying.

Leaning heavily on her crutches for emotional support more than anything else, she slowly resumed her
trek toward Prince. Cord Brannigan was due to arrive
within the hour. That didn't give her much time to say
goodbye to her friend.

SHARIF KNEW she was looking for trouble. He had been
right not to announce himself when he saw her leave
the bunkhouse, and instead, follow her out to the stables. The way she had concealed herself from the Colemans confirmed his suspicion. She had not given up
the idea of riding in the race.

Of course, he could not allow her to do such a foolish thing. No matter what means he employed.

Excitement sizzled in his veins at the thought of
what he was about to do. He glanced at his watch.
Omar would be almost ready for them. Unwittingly,
even Rose had lent a hand in Sharif's plan. Yet he had
a feeling, had she known what he was up to, she would
have approved.

From the shadows of the stables, he watched the
Colemans disappear toward the main house. No one

else was in sight. Most of the help were either preparing dinner, or washing up for the meal. He guessed it was no accident that Olivia had chosen this time to carry out whatever nefarious deed she had in mind.

However, what puzzled him was that she had not had someone saddle Prince. Sharif had already checked the stall. Yet it was impossible for her to accomplish the task herself. Her intentions made him all the more curious, and he waited only a few seconds before following her.

The eerie quiet gave him pause as he neared Prince's stall. Not even the other horses made any noise, and for a moment he wondered if Olivia was even present. And then he saw her, balancing on one crutch, her right arm wrapped around Prince's neck, her face buried, her shoulders shaking slightly…as though she were crying.

He stared, unable to move, barely able to breathe. Her pain may as well have been his own. It pressed against his chest like a boulder pinning him to a sheet of granite, squeezing his heart, robbing him of oxygen. That he heard not a sound from her, made the scene all that more difficult to bear.

He wanted to offer words of comfort, but he doubted they would be welcome. Perhaps she needed solitude to make peace with her new situation. Still, it was difficult for him not to go to her, to promise to chase the hurt away.

Sharif exhaled sharply. For the first time in his life, he tasted his own arrogance, and the flavor could not be more bitter. He did not have it in his power to help her. One of the things he admired most about Olivia was her strength. Whatever her ailment or problem, she would find her own solution. Without him.

Nevertheless, for the next three days, he would have her all to himself.

Chapter Fifteen

Livy knew she would never forget this day for as long as she lived. Nor would she forget the look of betrayal on Prince's face as Cord Brannigan led him away.

Staring at the mountainous stack of hundred-dollar bills in her hand, she knew it wasn't enough money. A million dollars wouldn't have been enough to make her feel any better. But thankfully this would help put a new roof on St. Mary's.

She had crawled into bed, intent on sleeping for a week, when she heard the knock at her door. Mumbling, she pulled a pillow over her head. She didn't care who it was. She didn't want to talk to anyone. Not even Rose, much as Livy had come to adore the woman.

And definitely not Shay. Not that she thought it was him. It was probably Mickey again, wanting to know if she'd changed her mind about eating dinner or playing poker. She hadn't. Maybe she wouldn't ever want to do anything fun again. That would be her penance for selling her friend. For foolishly hurting her ankle. For falling in love with the wrong man.

Her breath stuttered in her throat, and she pulled the pillow away from her face to get some air. Had she really done that? Had she gone and done something as stupid as fall in love?

Another knock. More persistent this time.

Love was such a big word. Huge. How did she know what it really meant? Of course she loved Father Michael and would do anything in her power for him. And she had great affection for all the Colemans. But love…as in *love*…

Her thoughts sprang to Shay and her pulse sped up, awareness creating energy in every pore. Just thinking about him made her feel different, more buoyant. But was this love?

And what about Shay? What did he think about what was happening? Did he even give the matter a thought at all?

The newspaper photo of him decking Corky Higgins came to mind, and she smiled for the first time in hours. Of course, she realized that meant nothing. Not to someone like Shay. But still, she'd never actually had anyone stand up for her before, not counting Seth Parker in the fifth grade, but only because he wanted her to help him with his homework.

The third angry knock shook the door. Which eliminated Rose and Mickey. Or anyone else for that matter. It had to be Shay.

"Go away." She rolled over to face the wall and pulled the pillow over her head again.

"I am coming in."

That should teach her to not lock the door. "I'm trying to sleep."

The door opened, but she didn't turn around. Her eyes and nose were probably red, and she just didn't feel like being social anyway. So she lay still, hardly breathing, until she heard the door close. And the lock click.

She flopped over and glared at him. "It's impolite to enter a woman's bedroom without being invited."

He didn't answer. He just stood there, his gaze sweeping the length of her body. Even though she was fully clothed in the same jeans and blue T-shirt she'd worn all day, she might as well have been naked the way he seemed so fascinated by her. And in spite of her miserable mood, her heart started to flutter with excitement.

"If you don't leave, I'll scream. Hopefully there'll be a reporter nearby." She turned completely over and raised herself on one elbow so that she could keep an eye on him.

Something was different about the way he was looking at her. Kind of that hint of longing Prince had when he thought she might have some sugar for him but he wasn't sure he'd get any. Even the way Shay stood was unusual. There was an indecisiveness, and maybe even a little fear in his stance. If she said boo, maybe he'd run.

Is that what she really wanted? Not that he would, but if she had her way? She swallowed and acknowledged the truth. The snugness of his jeans, and the way his open-neck shirt showed off his tanned chest made her want to lift the covers and pat the spot beside her in invitation. Which, for her, was utterly insane.

More than the sexy way he looked, she was touched by his desire to take care of her. No one other than Father Michael had ever wanted to do that, and she had to be careful not to read too much into Shay's attention.

"You think I care about reporters at this point?" He

glanced around the room. "Where is your medication?"

"What do you mean by *at this point?*"

"Your medication?"

"They're only painkillers. I don't need them anymore. What are you doing?" She scooted back against the wall when he reached into his pocket and pulled out a silk scarf.

"I hope you understand I have no intention of hurting you." He approached the bed and pulled out a second scarf. "However, your cooperation will be necessary in order to avoid any discomfort."

Panic clutched her insides and she cowered in the corner. He looked and sounded calm enough, but something in his eyes made her blood roar.

"Olivia." He lifted her chin. "Please, do not be afraid. I—I—" He shook his head and lowered his hand. "Now is not the time."

The fleeting emotions altering his features with dizzying speed caught her off balance and left her unprepared for his lightning move. Slipping a scarf over her mouth, he muffled her surprised gasp. When she struck out at him, he gathered her wrists in one hand and used the other scarf to tie them together.

She started to use her legs to kick free, but the pain delivered by the effort was enough to subdue her. When he scooped her up in his arms, she had little choice but to remain cradled against his chest, and pray that Mickey or anybody would have heard something and come to check it out.

"Olivia?"

She closed her eyes tight and refused to look at him. If he wanted her attention, he'd have to remove the scarves.

"Olivia," he said again, and hearing the amusement in his voice, she opened her eyes to glare at him with murderous intent. His lips curved. "You know I am not going to hurt you. We will be going for a short ride, and then I will free you."

She widened her eyes. She really hadn't thought about what he was going to do with her, but she didn't think he was going to take her anywhere. Automatically she started to object, but the scarf garbled her protests, and she ended up with an annoying tickle in her throat.

"Shh." Shay squeezed her a little tighter and briefly pressed his lips to her temple. "If you struggle, you may hurt your ankle."

She squinted at him, trying to look fierce.

He dipped his head and kissed her mouth through the scarf. Gently at first, then harder, as though he were as frustrated with the silk barrier as she amazingly was.

All thoughts of escape fled Livy and she clutched the front of his shirt, the silk around her wrists beginning to feel sensual rather than confining. Beneath her hands, his heart pounded and he staggered back a step.

She knew he wouldn't drop her. Oddly, she felt completely safe in his arms, even tied up as she was. If he removed her gag, she'd kiss him back, coax his tongue into her mouth. Wait for him to put his hand between her thighs again, let his fingers slip into the gathering dampness.

He pulled back from her mouth and her entire body mourned the retreat. But only for a moment, and then he bit the corner of the scarf and tried to pull it free with his teeth.

Anxious to help him, she lifted her bound hands, but he must have misunderstood and thought she was trying to get away. He stopped suddenly and reared his head back to look at her through glazed eyes.

She wished he'd remove the scarf and let her explain. Give her the chance to erase the disappointment forming on his face.

And then what?

Their physical attraction to each other had been obvious long before now. For a short time they could crawl into each other and forget their differences. But who would fill the hole left in her heart when he was gone?

She remained silent and still as he shifted her in his arms and eyed the scarves binding her wrists. He didn't have to worry—they were secure enough.

Resentment must have shown in her face because he looked away, and said, "We have only a short ride, and then you will be made comfortable."

He didn't say a word as he carried her out of the room and down the hall. Although she heard a television blaring from one of the rooms, not a soul was in sight, not even in the dining room where some of the guys usually played cards.

When they got outside, Shay's attendant waited with Zeus, a powerful black stallion Randy had recently purchased. No one else was around. Not near the stables and not toward the main house. How could the place look so deserted?

As they got closer, Livy stared pointedly at the other man, but he kept his gaze averted, even when Shay passed her to him while he mounted Zeus.

The two men never spoke a word. Once Shay was seated atop the horse, his attendant smoothly lifted her toward Shay's waiting arms. After she was again nestled against Shay's chest, they rode toward the lake where the sun was sinking into streams of pink and salmon.

Too many thoughts raced through her brain for her to think clearly enough about where they might be going. When they slowed to a walk near the guest house a few minutes later, her gut clenched. Of the two small houses on the Colemans' property, this one was the most isolated. It was also vacant and rarely used.

Her gaze slowly went from the house to Shay. He was watching her, his eyes a dark smoky-blue as he waited for her reaction. The scarf over her mouth was still damp from his kiss and goose bumps surfaced her flesh.

"You will be safe here," he finally said.

Panic gurgled in her chest. Was he kidding? She wasn't safe. Not with him. She did foolish things when he was around. And when they were alone, she was darn near hopeless.

He wasted no time in tying up Zeus, then carrying her to the door. It was already slightly ajar so that he only had to nudge it open. Once they got across the threshold, he kicked it shut.

She barely noticed. Her eyes widened at the inside of the cabin. She'd been here once before, but the living room looked nothing like she remembered it.

Sheer strips of cream-colored fabric draped the walls and were gathered at the center of the ceiling, giving it a tentlike look. All the furniture had been removed and the floor was covered with plush Persian carpets in burgundy and royal-blue. Large, velvety pillows with gold tassels were stacked and spread throughout the room. Several large vases of eucalyptus, white carnations and red roses scented the air, and off to the right was a small, low table laden with bowls of large, plump strawberries, ripe pears, mounds of whipped cream, and two trays of assorted cheeses.

Without a word, he carried her to a thick grouping of pillows and gently laid her down. Kneeling beside her, he removed first the scarf from her mouth, and then the one circling her wrists.

She watched as he inspected the skin where the scarves had bound her, fascinated by the way he carefully studied each side with genuine concern. And then he brought her wrists to his lips and pressed a string of slow, tiny kisses around to her palm.

Not once did she take her eyes off his face. She couldn't. He mesmerized her, tempted her to join in his dance of insanity. Except he would leave Texas soon, and she'd be left here to face the stares, struggling to ignore the whispers.

She yanked back her hand. "Why did you bring me here?"

Slowly he sank back on his heels and met her gaze. "To look after you."

"Who asked you?" She rubbed her wrists, not because they hurt, but because she needed to do something with her hands. "You had no right taking me like that."

"Would you have come had I asked?"

"Of course not."

He gave her a small tolerant smile and a lift of one eyebrow.

She shook her head at his arrogance. "You are genuinely amazing." When he chuckled, she added, "I didn't mean it as a compliment."

"Of that, I am well aware," he said, rising and forcing her to tilt her head back to look at him. "Have you been here before?"

She nodded and swept the room with another disbelieving glance.

"Then you know where the bath and bedroom are."

"I'm not staying here."

"Oh? And how do you propose to return?"

She glared at him. "You can't keep me here against my will. That's called kidnapping."

He shrugged. "You are still on the property, and of course, free to go. Anyway, I believe diplomatic immunity would protect me in the event of any misunderstanding."

"Misunderstanding my fanny. You know darn well I can't make it up that hill on crutches."

He shrugged again, and she'd have given just about anything to smack that smug face of his. "I will make a bargain with you. If, at the end of the three days, you still do not wish to be in my company, I will deliver you anywhere. I will even surrender myself to your authorities if that is what you want."

Her laugh was without humor. "Must be nice to have your overinflated confidence, but don't think I won't—" She blinked. "Three days? You're keeping me here for three days? Why?"

"Until the race is over."

It took a few seconds for his words to sink in, but when they did, sadness took some of the starch out of her. "You went to a lot of trouble for nothing. I won't be riding in the race."

"I will make certain of that."

She couldn't even laugh at the irony. If she tried, she might start sobbing again. "Like I said, you went to a lot of trouble for nothing."

He frowned and slowly lowered himself to her level. This time he sat on a pillow beside her. "I saw you sneaking around the stables earlier. Were you not trying to test your ability to ride?''

''You were spying on me?''

''No, I had gone to visit you when I saw you leave the bunkhouse and prowl around the stables.''

''I wasn't sneaking or prowling, you buffoon. I work there, remember?''

His frown deepened. ''Look at me.''

She lifted her chin so he could see her defiance. She had nothing to hide. At least, not anymore. Prince was gone. So were her dreams.

His gaze locked with hers. ''Tell me you were not doing anything secretive this afternoon.''

She blinked and started to lower her chin. He nudged it back up. ''Okay,'' she said through gritted teeth. ''I was at the stables on private business. But it had nothing to do with me riding in the race.''

He stared silently at her, as if waiting for some kind of admission. When none came, he asked, ''Why is this race so important to you?''

''You wouldn't understand.''

''I am surprised you are so quick to judge.''

''It doesn't matter anymore.'' She sighed, sick of thinking about the race and Prince and the orphanage. ''Not that you deserve it, but you have my word I won't even go near the start line. So let's just drop it.''

His troubled eyes searched her face, and afraid her expression would give too much away, she turned to look over the room. ''Do the Colemans know you did all this to their guest house?''

He didn't answer, and after a long prickly silence, she warily turned back to him. His eyebrows were drawn together in a thoughtful frown, and he seemed to be staring right through her.

"I will race in your place," he said finally.

"What? You can't." Was he kidding? Or insane. She searched his face for a clue. "You don't know the course. It covers some of the roughest terrain in the hill country."

"I have three days to learn."

He seemed so earnest she didn't know what to think. Not that any of it mattered. "Why would you do this?"

"Because it is important to you."

His words were soft and sincere and she stared back at him in confused silence. He was serious. Maybe he didn't understand the hazard involved for an unfamiliar rider...or maybe...

Dangerous thoughts tempted her. She should let the matter drop, explain that the race no longer meant anything to her. But the tender way he was looking at her made her want to hear more. "Shay." She touched his hand. "You don't realize how risky this race can be for someone who doesn't know the territory. But I do appreciate your offer. Really, I do."

"I have been riding since I was old enough to climb atop a horse. Do not underestimate me."

"I'm not. I'm just trying to make you understand."

"I am not a total fool. I intend to ride Prince. He already knows the course. Besides, I assume the reason for your determination is to showcase him."

Oh, God, she didn't want to talk about Prince, or explain why he was no longer in the stables. "Can we just drop it? I already told you I won't try to ride in the race."

He held on to her hand when she tried to withdraw it. "Something is wrong. What is it?"

She sighed. "You're holding me here against my

will. I'd say that pretty much makes this a not so average day.''

Shay continued to stare at her until she had to look away.

With a finger hooked under her chin, he brought her gaze back to his. ''Why would it matter to you if I race? I would think you would hope for me to break my neck.''

''That's not true.''

''So what is it?''

His voice was low and caring, his eyes concerned, and she was afraid the tears would come again. She bit her lower lip, trying to think of the right response. The one that would shut him up, make him leave her alone.

Anger and regret and grief had simmered in her chest for the past two hours and if she didn't do something quickly, she just might explode.

''Olivia?''

She swallowed, took a deep breath and an amazing calm came over her. ''There won't be any race for Prince. I sold him today.''

Chapter Sixteen

Sharif stared at the resignation in her dull violet eyes, and was at a total loss for words. Keeping hold of one cold hand, he took her other one and tried to warm them between his. She offered no resistance, simply let him rub her lifeless fingers. Her lack of fighting spirit spoke volumes.

"Will you tell me about it?" he asked.

She gave a small shrug. "Nothing to tell. I needed some money and Prince sold for a good price."

His chest constricted. She looked so brave even as she stuttered over the word *price*. "If it was only money you needed, why did you not come to me?"

She tried to withdraw her hands. He held tight. "Why would I do that? I hardly know you."

Her words were like an arrow to his heart. Except they were the truth. So why did they feel so wrong? Why had his heart taken such personal offense? "Have you so easily forgotten this morning?"

A rosy pink seeped into her complexion, and she again tried to free her hands...and succeeded. "I'm sure what happened this morning is common for you, but it isn't for me." She looked down and picked at the hem of her shirt. "I'm not proud of the way—"

"No." At his abrupt tone, her head came back up, and their eyes met. "Do not speak of mistakes or regrets. If I have any regret at all, it is that I did not make love to you."

Her color heightened. "We did, sort of," she mumbled, then her eyes widened before she closed them, and groaned. "I have to go to the bathroom."

He smiled, then leaned forward to kiss her eyelids. She promptly lifted them. "It was not my intention to embarrass you," he said, and felt a stirring of something foreign inside his chest. He shifted uncomfortably as the truth sunk in. "The way you made me feel this morning was not common to me at all."

A startled look crossed her face, and then her gaze narrowed. "Save the sweet talk. You've already made sure I'm not going anywhere."

"Which means I have no reason to speak lies."

She blinked, then stared at him as if trying to measure his sincerity. "I don't know what you want from me, Shay, but whatever it is I don't have it to give."

"You can tell me why you needed the money."

"Why? What does it matter now?"

Sharif exhaled loudly. She was the most difficult female he had ever met. "It matters to me."

"Not good enough." She folded her arms across her chest in that defiant manner he both admired and loathed.

"Prince is your friend," he said, regretting that he made her flinch. "You would only sell him if you were in trouble."

She got up on her knees and tried to reach for the crutches he had left against the wall near the door. They were too far and she started to crawl toward them.

"Olivia." He dove after her, annoyed with himself that he had clearly caused her pain. "Please."

He heard her sniff as he circled an arm around her waist and pulled her toward him. Unprepared for her outburst, he narrowly missed the fist she flung at him, and he ended up on his back with her on top of him.

"You're really beginning to tick me off," she said, glaring at him, her nose red, her eyes slightly glassy. Then she tried twisting off, and when she failed, she slumped against him and laid her head on his chest.

Her capitulation was more a result of wanting to avoid his gaze than actual surrender, he realized. But for whatever the reason, he was glad she had quit struggling.

Sighing, he rested his chin on top of her head and stroked her back. "Why must you fight me at every turn?"

"Don't take it personally. It's a habit."

He smiled a little, until he realized what she meant. Life had never been easy for her. No parents, no family, no security. She had fought her own battles. As a child, uncertainty and change had colored her future. As an adult, all she'd had was Prince. Now he was gone.

She would be horrified, he knew, if she realized how much she had just told him with her simple statement. And he was horrified at how much her pain was getting to him. How much *she* was getting to him.

Olivia was right. He had a history of many women, but until today, he had always thought only of his own gratification. This morning his energy and need had been focused entirely on giving her pleasure. The realization unnerved him.

After silently stroking her back for several minutes,

he asked, "Is it so difficult to believe that I care about you? About what drove you to sell Prince?"

She stiffened. "Stop saying his name."

"Okay." He kissed her hair and slowly coaxed her into relaxing by running his hand down to the curve of her buttocks and back up again. "We will not talk at all."

She shifted her slight weight, her hip and thigh rubbing him intimately, and to his disgust, he began to harden. She must have felt his arousal because she stiffened suddenly. "Fine."

"Fine?" His concentration had dissolved.

"You said we wouldn't talk, and I said, fine."

"Yes, fine."

She moved again, and this time he knew he had to do something. It was a shame, because it was nice having her so close without her struggling to get away from him, but it was not his intention to get physical. At least not this soon.

Taking her by the shoulders, he gently put her away from him, while bringing them both to sitting positions. Unprepared for the maneuver, she ended up straddling him, the pressure she put on his groin nearly sending him into a cold sweat.

He had to get her off him immediately but, wary of her injured ankle, he hesitated. And looked into her troubled eyes. It was a mistake he recognized instantly, but it was too late. He was already drowning.

"I, uh…" She visibly swallowed. "I wasn't sure what you were doing. Um, I guess I'm hurting you," she said, but made no move to lift herself.

When her gaze lowered to his mouth and she leaned forward slightly, Sharif held his breath. Not a damn thing could be done about the granite forming beneath his fly. She had to feel it. Did she know what she was doing?

He remained still, waiting to see what she would do next, but she seemed shy suddenly, uncertain. And then she rolled off and scooted back to sit on a blue velvet cushion.

With nothing to block the view, the bulge in his pants was obvious and her wide-eyed gaze was riveted to the spot. Not much could be done without embarrassing her, so he ignored her stare and casually got to his feet.

"May I get you something to drink?" he asked, and waited for her reluctant eyes to meet his.

She nodded. "Something cold."

"Yes," he agreed, and gratefully walked toward the bar. He had never been modest or timid about his body or his sexuality, but with Olivia everything seemed off balance. He had the oddest desire to protect her. Even from himself.

He fixed them each a drink and took them over to her with a plate of cheese and crackers. She took a big gulp before he could stop her, and she went into a fit of coughing.

He took the drink from her and placed a hand on her back. She was so tiny, much more fragile than he was accustomed to, and his protective instinct surged anew.

"There is vodka in the orange juice," he said, when her coughs subsided.

"No kidding." She coughed again. "You could've warned me."

"My apologies."

"My fanny."

He smiled. "I thought it would relax you."

"Sleeping in my own bed, in my own room, would

relax me." She cast a peevish glance around the room. "This looks like the inside of a tent."

"Do you like it?"

She shrugged and tried to look indifferent, but the twinkle in her eyes said otherwise. "It's okay."

"It was in the desert in a tent such as this that my father proposed to my mother."

"Rose?"

He saw the challenge in her face, and he took a sip of his own drink. "Queen Nadirah." He set the glass aside and added, "You forget I have two mothers."

A smile touched the corners of her mouth and her face lit up. His acceptance of Rose obviously pleased her. "You're very lucky."

"Yes, and I look forward to my mother telling me the story of how she became betrothed to my birth father."

Olivia smiled broadly. "I already know, and it's very romantic."

He could watch her all night. The way one side of her mouth always lifted a second before the other, and the way her eyes glowed when she was excited or happy. "Tell me," he said when he realized his attention was making her uncomfortable.

"Oh no. Your mom has to do that." She started to reach for her glass again but left it untouched.

He got her some plain orange juice, then sat beside her. "I have a confession to make."

She eyed him warily. "Do I want to hear this?"

He gestured around the room. "All of this, I had planned for your seduction."

Her eyebrows shot up, and panic crossed her face before she regained her composure. "And?"

Sharif smiled. "I have changed my mind."

"Why?"

"I thought you would be pleased," he said, damn pleased himself at the brief disappointment in her eyes.

She straightened. "I am. Of course. I'm thrilled. I—I'm just surprised."

"You think I no longer want you?"

"No. I mean, I don't know." Color stained her cheeks and she exhaled a huff of air. "I'm surprised you're telling me this, is all. Darn it! I told you I didn't want to hear it."

"Shall I stop?"

"There's more?"

He gave a noncommittal shrug. "Nothing that important. The evening will run its course regardless."

She drummed her fingers on the velvet cushion. Then she picked up her orange juice, took a sip and set it back down. She stretched her neck from side to side, scratched her chin, idly looked around, then brought her gaze to his. "Okay, tell me."

"Are you sure?"

She gave him a dirty look.

He smiled again. "I have decided to wait for you to seduce me."

Squinting, she strained forward a little, her head tilting slightly to the side as though she were having trouble hearing. "You expect me to—to make a move on you?"

"Expecting is not quite the correct word. Hoping is more accurate. In the meantime, we will talk. Tell me about your childhood."

Disbelief clouded her face, then suspicion. "This is a trick, right?"

He shook his head, careful to keep eye contact. He wanted no doubt from her, only trust.

"Where are you going with this?" she asked. "You don't still have this crazy notion of adding me to a harem."

"The truth? I have no idea." By the sudden anger on her face he realized he had misspoken, and he held up a hand. "First, I have no harem, and I have since been disavowed of considering one. However, our relationship or where we are going is as mysterious to me as a mirage in the desert."

He watched her nibble her lower lip while contemplating his admission, and felt somewhat guilty he had withheld something. He suspected that in his heart of hearts he knew exactly where their relationship was headed. But he still found the idea difficult to fathom. Even more than that, the prospect of forever after was alarming.

Yet not half as unpalatable as the thought of not seeing Olivia again.

"Okay," she finally said, "we'll talk, but it has to go both ways."

He nodded his agreement, and she said, "You first."

His initial reaction was to balk. He did not share his thoughts or anything personal with anyone, but seeing the doubt in her face, he knew too much weighed on his willingness to participate.

Sharif cleared his throat. Not a single thought came to mind. "Perhaps you should go first."

She gave him a condescending smile. "No, you started this. You go. And if you say you think the Cowboys will make it to the Super Bowl, I'm gonna throw something."

He had no idea what she was talking about, but he cleared his throat again, struggling for a profound thing to say. "All right, I did not want to meet Rose...my mother."

"Really?" She reared her head back in exaggerated shock, and annoyance needled him. "That's almost as bad as predicting the Super Bowl."

"May I finish?" he asked with indignation, even though he had not planned to add anything else.

"I beg your pardon," she said. "Please continue."

At her flip tone, he started to get annoyed again, but then he noticed the anxious way she was unconsciously straining forward, the way she could not still her fingers. The fear in her eyes. As though what he had to say would determine the fate of the world. Or at least their fate.

"When I discovered that my sister, Serena, was adopted, I was stunned. I pitied her, but I was relieved it was her and not I who was the outcast." He shook his head. "Perhaps that is not the correct word."

"I understand. You didn't want to be different."

"Yes, that was part of it, but nevertheless I quickly found myself..." He waved a hand, unable to translate his thoughts. "As you Americans would say, in the hot seat. All my life I was one person, and then suddenly I was someone else altogether."

Olivia gasped. "No, you weren't. That's ridiculous. You were still the same person, the only difference was that you had two other people who loved you as much as your parents."

He smiled at her naiveté. "Parents who did not have the same bloodlines."

Her eyebrows drew together in confusion. "But that doesn't make you a different person." She blinked, and her thoughtful frown turned thunderous. "It makes you a snob. Are you saying being Rose's son isn't good enough?''

His defenses shot up. "You are not knowledgeable about matters concerning royalty."

"And if you don't consider yourself damn lucky to have Rose as a mother, then you don't have the brains of a jackass."

He snorted. "You ask me to share my thoughts and then you criticize."

"Yeah, well…" She folded her arms across her chest, looking a little sheepish. But then she added, "Those were stupid thoughts."

Anger sizzled in his veins. "At least I opened up. When I asked you about Prince, you shut me out."

Color drained from her face, and he immediately regretted bringing up the subject. She uncrossed her arms and visibly swallowed. "I had to sell him," she whispered. "I promised Father Michael a new roof."

"For the orphanage?"

She nodded, her eyes growing suspiciously bright. "That's why I needed the prize money. Without the repairs, St. Mary's may have had to close."

But Prince? A blind man could see she loved that horse. Sharif was again momentarily speechless. Stampeding camels could not have inflicted more pain than he felt at the brave lift of her chin. "You could have come to me. There had to be another way—"

She shook her head. "I take care of my own problems. Besides, it's over. And I know Cord Brannigan will give—" her breath caught, and he could see her silent struggle to compose herself "—Prince a good home." She lifted her half-filled glass of orange juice. "May I have some more?"

Understanding her need for privacy, he said nothing

as he stood and took the glass. He lingered at the bar, trying to give her time. He longed to comfort her, hoped he had the right words. With every layer of Olivia's personality and character that peeled away, an unfamiliar yearning in him grew, a yearning for intimacy, a yearning for Olivia.

"Hey, I'm getting pretty thirsty over here."

He topped off her glass and returned to her, surprised at how quickly she had recovered. Her voice was still a little thin and her complexion wan, but she gave him a faint smile.

Their gazes stayed entwined as he handed her the glass, then sat on a cushion in front of her. "I am truly sorry about—"

She put a finger to his lips, silencing him. "It's okay. I'm glad I told you. Thanks for listening."

Before she could lower her hand, he covered it with his and pressed a kiss in her palm. "You are the most noble person I know."

She promptly withdrew. "No, I'm not."

This time he put a silencing finger to her lips. "You performed an incredibly noble and unselfish act."

She shook her head. "No. I simply did the only thing I knew to do."

For the first time in his life, Sharif realized that a woman could break his heart. He smiled at her, his chest already beginning to tighten. "That is precisely what makes you noble."

She stared back at him, looking a little confused, a little frightened. He wanted to kiss her so badly it took all of his control to not lean toward her. She was too vulnerable, and it would be unfair of him to foster intimacy.

She blinked, cleared her throat. "I have a question."

She hesitated, and he took her hand. "Why haven't you kissed me yet?"

That startled a laugh out of him. "Well…" He floundered, unsure how to explain himself without upsetting her.

"I get it." She nodded sagely. "I have to do the seducing." Casting a look at her wrapped ankle, she made a face. "Could you help me out and get a little closer?"

Sharif rubbed the tension starting at the back of his neck. "Olivia, perhaps this is not the time."

Confusion and hurt clouded her face, and she shrunk back. "Oh…okay."

"You misunderstand. I want very much to kiss you but—"

"You don't have to say that."

"Precisely." He laughed wryly, and she narrowed her gaze, but it was with himself he found amusement. "For maybe the first time in my life, I am trying to be noble. You are distraught over Prince…"

The uncertainty on her face cleared, and her lips started to curve as she leaned forward.

"…and it would be wrong for me to— Be careful of your ankle."

She had gotten to her knees and grabbed a hold of his shirt. She tugged him toward her, and their lips met awkwardly. In spite of his good intentions, he had an immediate reaction to her touch, her feminine scent, and he kissed her more fervently than he should have.

"Olivia," he whispered when he had enough power to pull away. "We should not—"

He stopped and swallowed hard when she pulled her shirt out from the waistband of her jeans and started unbuttoning it. By the time the third button was unfas-

tened, he could see the slight swell between the cups
of her plain white cotton bra.

"Olivia," he repeated, his voice hoarse, barely ser-
viceable. "You do not know what—"

"Shut up, Shay." Her trembling fingers faltered with
the last button, and then she freed it and shrugged off
her shirt. "You're right—I don't know what I'm doing,
so bear with me."

She took a deep breath, her breasts rising and falling,
as she reached behind and unclasped her bra. It fell,
displaying twin small firm mounds, crowned with rosy
nipples.

Sharif's entire body tightened with need. He tried to
force his gaze higher, but he was hopelessly trapped
by the sheer beauty of her.

She squirmed, looking as though she were about to
cover herself. "Aren't you supposed to take your shirt
off about now?" she asked in a small, hesitant voice.

"I think so," he said, dragging his gaze up to meet
hers. He lied, he realized, as he tore at the buttons of
his shirt. Thinking was an impossibility.

A shy smile curved her lips, then she lowered her
eyes to his exposed chest. "You're gonna have to help
me along here."

At the nervous quaver in her voice, he reached for
her hand and placed it palm side down against the skin
above his left nipple. Her eyes widened as his heart
slammed wildly against her hand. "You do that to
me," he said softly. "I am yours. All yours."

With shaky fingers, she picked up his hand and
placed it over her breast, her nipple pearling against his
palm. Her other nipple hardened, as well, and he leaned
in for a taste.

At first she stiffened, and then with a slight whimper

she swayed toward him, and he eagerly took her into his mouth, his hunger for her erasing almost everything else from his mind. The only thought he held on to was how much he wanted her, not just in his bed, but in his life.

Olivia seemed to go boneless in his arms, and he gently laid her back against the velvet pillows, his greed barely allowing him to release her sweet taste. When he unsnapped her jeans and drew down the zipper, and then slid the denim down her thighs, she hardly moved. She smiled lazily at him, a dreamy look in her eyes. But when he started to remove her white panties, she stiffened again. Immediately he stopped.

"It's okay," she whispered. "I'm just a little nervous."

"Me, too," he said, which was, amazingly, the truth. At her skeptical look, he added, "I want this to be right."

He rolled his shoulders back, freeing his arms from the sleeves, and let his shirt slide to the floor. Then he removed his pants, while watching her stare at him in total fascination. When he slid off his black silk boxers, her eyes widened, and she gripped the sides of the pillow until her knuckles whitened.

Slowly he lowered himself beside her. He was probably the first naked man she had seen and he knew he had to take care not to alarm her. He gently splayed his hand across her belly, letting two of his fingers slip beneath the elastic of her panties. She tensed for a moment, then shifted her hips, allowing his fingers to slip further inside.

And then she cupped his face with one hand and kissed him.

Seconds later, her other hand found his arousal. Sharif sucked in a breath. Any more pressure and he would explode. He quickly removed her panties and found the wetness awaiting him. She made tiny sounds of contentment and spread her thighs farther apart. He suckled her breasts, trailed kisses up her throat, captured her lips. She tasted so sweet and inviting he thought he might embarrass himself.

He moved a little to defuse her eagerness, but his excitement only rose. He dared not tell her to slow down for fear she would take it as personal criticism. Still, if he did not get her to…

Groaning out loud, he clamped a hand over hers. "Olivia—"

She stilled. "Am I hurting you?"

"Killing me."

Smiling, she resumed her pace. Until Sharif was forced to pull away. He fumbled in the pocket of his discarded trousers, found the foil packet, then sheathed himself while she looked on in fascination.

The look of complete trust she gave him as he spread her thighs wider and positioned himself between them would forever humble him. There were so many more things he had to say to her. Ways he had to please her. But for now they would become one.

Her eyes stayed open as he slowly slid into her. He stopped when he met with resistance, and kissed the tip of her nose. When he started to warn her it might hurt a little, she silenced him with a finger to his lips and, with her beautiful violet eyes, begged him to continue.

He took the final plunge. Nothing on earth had prepared him for the sensation of losing himself in her. He knew instantly there was nothing he would not do for this woman. She owned him now, body and soul.

Chapter Seventeen

Livy's ankle started to ache, but she tried to ignore it. She was having such a wonderful dream she wasn't ready to wake up yet. Something scratched the side of her cheek, and when she shifted away from the source, a lot more than her ankle ached. Her entire body felt strange, and then she remembered last night, and her eyes flew open.

It was still early morning, judging by the soft light seeping into the room and casting muted shadows on the velvet pillows scattered around her. She saw the indentation on the red one where Shay had lain beside her, but there was no sign of him.

She stretched out again and closed her eyes, smiling, knowing he was probably in the kitchen trying to make coffee or mix orange juice or doing some other mundane task that took him three times as long as anyone else.

They'd had an incredible night. She'd seen a side to him that could make frozen butter melt. Not just the physical attention he'd paid to her, but how he'd waited on her, tended to her every need, even though it was obvious that half the time he had no idea what he was doing.

She stretched out some of the kinks and listened for him. No noise came from the kitchen. "Shay?" She frowned, waited a couple of minutes, then called out again.

No answer.

A chill crawled up her spine and she swept a gaze around the room, searching for a note. Anything that would explain why he'd suddenly left her. There had to be an explanation. After all the wonderful things he'd said last night...the intimacy they'd reached... there was no way he'd just...

She swallowed and forced herself up to a sitting position. The room that had looked so whimsical and beautiful minutes ago seemed to be closing in on her.

"Shay?" she called out a little louder, and glanced around for signs of him. It looked as though he'd never even been here.

She struggled to her knees and grabbed her crutches. Funny, they'd been leaning against the far wall last night. Shay had to have moved them closer. Was this his way of telling her to leave before he got back? She didn't want to believe it of him, couldn't believe it. Not after all the sweet promises he'd made. But what did she really know about men? How could she have thought someone as sophisticated as Shay would want her?

Old insecurities clawed at her raw emotions, and she ruthlessly batted them away. She'd worked hard to not believe she'd been a discard. Father Michael had worked even harder to help her see that being abandoned was not her fault. She owed it to him not to fold now, but it was hard. Really hard.

But where was Shay? Why hadn't he at least left her a note?

After two failed attempts, she got to her feet, dressed, and hobbled to the door. It would be a miracle if she made it uphill to the bunkhouse without busting up her other ankle, but she couldn't stay here, either. Shay may have broken her heart, but she still had her pride.

"BUT, MOM, YOU DON'T KNOW HIM like I do. The man is impossible." Jessica's annoyed voice carried down the hall, and Livy cursed under her breath and stopped cold. She was hoping to catch Jessica alone in the ranch office.

"I've known Nick Grayson since he was born," Vi said, a smile in her voice. "I'd say I know him pretty darn well."

"Yeah, well, he treats you a whole lot nicer than he treats me," Jessica mumbled. "I can't believe you and Dad are forcing me to work with him in Dallas."

Livy groaned to herself. This was the second time she'd ended up eavesdropping unintentionally. She had started to turn around when she heard the door slam at the other end of the hall. It didn't matter who it was, she didn't want to see anyone but Jessica, so she hid as best she could. Unfortunately, Jessica and her mother's conversation could still be overheard.

"We're not forcing you to work with Nick," Vi was saying. "We're only asking you to give it a chance. You know your father hopes someday you'll take his place at Coleman-Grayson, but you have to learn more about the business. Nick can help you."

Jessica started to protest, but Vi cut her off. "Wait— before you say anything, all we're proposing is a three-month trial starting in October after the horse show nationals. If it doesn't work out, then we drop it."

Livy welcomed the brief silence and sagged against the wall. Jessica was going to be in no mood to listen to Livy's problems. Her friend had complained about Nick enough that Livy suspected there might be something brewing between the two of them. Of course Jessica had hotly denied it. Nick was just as stubborn. Men. What a thorn in the backside.

"Only three months?" Jessica asked finally. "And you all won't bug me about Nick anymore?"

"Honey, this isn't about Nick," Vi said softly. "This is about work."

Livy winced. She could just picture Jessica's face flaming redder than a ripe August tomato.

"Of course," Jessica mumbled. "I guess I can do it for three months. Now, can we talk about the budget?"

No one had come down the hall since the door slammed, and Livy poked her head out for a look. The only person who knew she was here was Mickey, because he'd found her trudging up the hill and given her a ride. As curious as he was, she'd sworn him to secrecy and she trusted him not to tell anyone where she was.

But now what? She'd wanted to talk to Jessica. Actually, Livy really wanted to talk to Rose. But that was out of the question. She was Shay's mother, and right now, Livy didn't have many kind things to say about him.

A lump formed in her throat, thinking about last night. He'd said they would be together forever. He'd said he loved her. Maybe she was jumping to conclusions. But why hadn't he left a note? It would have made all the difference.

Part of the problem was she'd read those damn tabloids Mickey had shown her. All of them were filled with pictures of glamorous women Shay had dated. And dumped. Livy hadn't paid too much attention at the time. She thought those kinds of papers were awful, but now, the reports of his womanizing hammered her brain.

How could she have possibly believed he was interested in her? Plain ol' Olivia Smith, who didn't even know her real name, because her parents hadn't bothered to leave a note, either.

To her horror, a sob broke loose and Livy nearly fell over her crutches in an attempt to stifle it. She grabbed the one crutch just in time before it smashed against the wall and woke the dead. Positioning herself for flight, she turned and nearly ran into Rose.

"Livy? What are you doing here?"

"I, um, was looking for Jessica, but she's busy."

Rose narrowed her gaze in concern. "Are you all right?"

"Sure." Livy tried to smile.

Rose looked unconvinced. "You look a little pale," she said, and Livy shrugged it off. "Well…" Rose's brows drew together, and she glanced at the folded piece of paper in her hand. "I'm looking for Sharif, have you seen him?"

Livy couldn't speak at first. "Not today," she finally said, her voice sounding unnatural.

Rose frowned, indecision dulling her eyes. "Come on, Livy, let's go to my room," she said, with a resigned sigh. "It's time we had a talk."

SHARIF BURST INTO the foyer of the main house like an angry bull. No one was in sight. Just like at the bunkhouse. Where the hell was everybody?

Where the hell was Olivia?

He went to the first-floor bathroom and splashed some cold water on his face. He was hot, his neck damp with perspiration, more from nerves than the heat.

Olivia was not in the guest house, nor in her room. He had been gone a little over an hour. How far could she have gotten on crutches? Why had she left in the first place?

Worrying about someone, and feeling utterly helpless, was a new experience for him. He did not much care for it. But that did not make the feeling go away. He was stuck with it, and the only way he saw to overcome it was to keep Olivia by his side for the rest of his life. But first he had to find her.

He left the washroom and headed for the kitchen. Someone, Ella, he thought her name was, usually stayed pretty close to the stoves near mealtimes and it was almost noon. Before he got there, he saw his father on the phone in the den.

As soon as King Zak spotted him, he waved Sharif to him, the urgency in his face warring with Sharif's desire to keep going in search of Olivia.

His father quickly replaced the receiver. "We have been looking for you."

"Have you seen Olivia?"

King Zak eyed him consideringly. "About an hour ago. Come with me. Rose has a letter you must read."

"I have to see Olivia first. Where is she?"

His father had already started out of the room, but he stopped and frowned with disapproval when he saw that Sharif had made no attempt to follow. "Now? I have no idea. However, your mother awaits you with some urgent news."

"Where did you see Olivia?"

"She was with Rose."

Sharif hesitated, noting the smile that lurked at the corners of his father's mouth. He was one of the kindest, most intelligent men Sharif knew. He could also be cunning. "All right," Sharif said finally, "we will go see Rose."

They had almost made it to the housekeeper's suite where Rose lived when it occurred to Sharif that he was not the least bit curious about the news they wanted to give him. He only wanted to see Olivia. To know she was safe. To understand why she had run away.

"Sharif? Where have you been?" Rose was leaving her suite as they approached. She glanced at King Zak. "Have you told him about the letter?"

Impatience pricked Sharif. "Is Olivia here?"

"She was…" Rose said, her tone vague, as she glanced again at King Zak. "Why don't you two come in?"

Sharif followed her inside, barely able to hold on to his patience. "Before anyone says another word, I want to see Olivia."

Rose gestured to a pink floral sofa. "Livy is fine, and you'll see her in due time. Right now there is an important matter that needs addressing."

The sternness in her voice and expression caught him off guard, and he said nothing while she went to an antique desk in the corner and withdrew an envelope from the drawer. At least he knew Olivia was all right. Still, his uneasiness did not abate.

"I have a letter here from Azzam, your father's brother. You need to read it." Rose handed him the envelope.

He unfolded the letter. It was several pages long. "What is this about?"

"It is best if you read it for yourself," his father said.

"On second thought," Rose said suddenly, "Sharif seems to be in a bit of a hurry, so maybe we could give him a quick summary and he can read the letter later."

King Zak stared at her as if she had just gone mad. But Rose only smiled, and King Zak lifted an eyebrow, his curious gaze not leaving her.

"Please, sit," she said, and expansively gestured toward the sofa again, except this time, her hand caught a large decorative urn, and it went crashing to the floor. "Oh, how clumsy of me."

She put a hand to her throat, but oddly, she did not look very upset. And when both Sharif and his father jumped to pick up the pieces, she waved a dismissive hand. "Don't bother. I'll tend to it later. Let's sit."

Sharif and his father exchanged glances. King Zak obviously thought she was acting a little peculiar, too, but they both did as she asked, and she took a seat across from them.

"Basically, this letter explains what happened thirty years ago. Some of it we already know, some we suspected, and now we have confirmation that it was Azzam's wife, Layla, who was solely responsible for the assassination of your father and—" her expression and voice softened "—taking you away from me.

"Apparently, Layla saw the news reports about my return to the States, how your brothers are all alive and well, and that King Zak and the people of Balahar know the truth about your parentage, and she snapped. She publicly confessed that she was behind the assassination of your father. She was enraged that her husband had not inherited the throne, and not having any sons, she knew they would never have the power she wanted.''

''Azzam knew nothing of this?'' Sharif asked.

''He learned some of this months ago, but he didn't know about you. He's sickened by the entire revelation.'' Rose stared evenly into Sharif's eyes. ''He is ready to step aside and acknowledge you as king of Sorajhee.''

''Me? Sorajhee?'' Stunned, his mind went numb. He knew he would someday rule Balahar, but Sorajhee?

Rose's gaze never wavered. She was a strong woman. No wonder she had survived all those years in the sanitarium. He respected and admired her even more at this moment.

''You are their true king,'' she said. ''You are your father's son.''

Sharif glanced at King Zak. Not a muscle moved in his face. He understood their relationship was not threatened. To his shame, only Sharif had fostered doubt. ''What about Alex? He is firstborn. Or even Mac or Cade?''

She shook her head with a smile. ''Their roots are here in Texas now. It's you, Sharif, who belongs as head of Sorajhee.''

Fears and hopes collided inside his head. There was so much to consider. There was…

He turned abruptly to King Zak. He was no longer a young man. They spoke more and more of the time Sharif would succeed him. ''But Balahar is my home.''

King Zak smiled. ''Yes, son, it will always be your home. That is why I am agreeing to a union between Balahar and Sorajhee.''

"Will our people accept this alliance?"

"Make no mistake. This is not a sentimental decision. United we will become too strong for our enemies to the east to attempt a takeover." King Zak eyed him with concern. "Ruling both countries fairly and to the satisfaction of everyone is a tremendous responsibility. We would not ask this of you if we did not feel you were capable. However, are you ready?"

Sharif stared out the window. He understood his father's implication. Accepting leadership meant his entire life would change. No more jet-setting on whim. No more escapades that would land him in the tabloids.

Oddly, the thought did not bother him. The all-night parties, the swank international club scene, mindless days of baccarat and fine wine now seemed like a lifetime ago. They held no appeal. Because, he strongly suspected, of Olivia.

Panic coiled in his belly. What would accepting this new role mean to their future together? His mother was an American—just like Olivia.

He looked at Rose. She was watching him with a speculative frown. He did not yet know her well enough to predict what she was thinking, but he knew in his heart he could count on her support.

She got up from the sofa, and he had the strangest feeling she was trying to avert his gaze. "You understand, of course, this makes your relationship with Livy rather sticky," she said, as she paced across the room, careful to avoid the pieces of shattered urn. "You have the subjects of two countries anticipating your every move. And lest you forget, Livy is a commoner. It would be difficult to make her your queen."

Disbelief stung his ears. Disappointment cramped his heart. He smiled without humor and sadly nodded his head. "You are absolutely right, Mother," he said, and was startled to see his disappointment mirrored in her eyes. "It would be very difficult. Olivia already is a queen."

He looked at King Zak, daring him to refute his claim. "She is noble and wise and kind. If she will honor me with her hand in marriage, I have no doubt she will always put our people's welfare before her own. And I will be the luckiest and happiest man in all of Balahar and Sorajhee."

Sharif's gaze strayed out the window, a wry twist to his mouth. How different the rolling Desert Rose pasture looked today. Full of endless promise. Olivia helped him look toward the future, leaving the past where it belonged. "I had once thought she was not worthy of me. Ironic, is it not?" He returned his attention to Rose. "It is I who am not worthy of her."

His mother's brilliant smile lightened his heart. "I think you just proved that you are."

The shrewd gleam in her eyes aroused his suspicion. "Be warned," he said, glancing between her and the strangely silent King Zak, "if the people do not accept Olivia as their queen, they will have to find a new king."

A noise in the bedroom drew their attention. The door opened, and Olivia stood in the doorway. Her eyes were bright and shining, her hair sticking out in a hundred places. How much had she heard? Most of it, judging by the slight trembling of her lips.

She shrugged a little, her cheeks reddening. "A loud crash woke me."

Sharif looked at the shattered urn, then at Rose. A devious smile curved her mouth. She knew he would defend Olivia, and she wanted Olivia to hear it.

He swallowed hard, more nervous than he had ever remembered being in his life. His gaze drew back to the woman he loved more than life itself.

She put her hands on her hips. "Are you going to do it right this time?" Using her crutches and awkwardly stepping around the shards of urn, she came toward him, then stopped just out of reach. "You don't have to get on one knee or anything, but you have to ask nicely. And if you mention one word about first or second wife, I will have to deck you."

Sharif bit back a smile, his heart pounding so hard it hurt.

"Olivia Smith?" He took a step forward. "Will you do me the honor of being my wife? My queen? Forever and ever?"

She patted her hair. "Will I have to wear a crown?"

He laughed. "Only if you wish."

Her lips lifted in a mischievous grin, and she presented her hand, knuckles up, ready to be kissed. "Okay."

He pulled her toward him and wrapped his arms around her. Her chin automatically lifted as she waited for his kiss. "I love you," he murmured against her mouth. "I will always love you."

"I love you." Her voice was breathless, her eyes wide and bright. Her heart pounded against his chest.

"Oh, my goodness." Rose half sighed, half sobbed. "Do I get to plan the wedding?"

King Zak slid an arm around her and drew her to his side. "You may plan two."

Rose's worried gaze flew from King Zak to Sharif.

Startled at first, Sharif briefly studied his father's relaxed features. Something had sparked between them from the beginning, Sharif knew, but he had not expected the announcement.

He smiled. "I hope this is not your way of asking her, Father. I can tell you from experience you are in monumental trouble."

Everyone laughed.

"I asked her this morning, and she agreed." King Zak met his eyes. "Provided you approve."

"Of course he does," Olivia said, happy tears in her eyes. She elbowed him in the ribs. "Tell them."

"Yes, my queen," he said, bowing with a straight face. This would be life with Olivia. He could not wait.

Olivia smiled happily at Rose and King Zak. "Maybe we could have a double wedding?"

"It may be too complicated for that—" King Zak began.

"I know." Rose clasped her hands together. "You and Sharif can get married here so the family can give you a big Texas wedding. And then you can have another ceremony in Balahar. With us."

King Zak nodded slowly, obviously considering the social and political imports.

Sharif looked at Olivia. "What do you think?"

She wrapped her arms around his neck. "I think I'm dreaming."

"Better wake up. I have a surprise for you." He tugged her hand, then ignored her excited questions all the way down the hall and out the front door.

"There's something you'd better know about me," she said, breathless with anticipation and from trying to keep up with him. "You can't tell me there's a surprise, and then—"

They had just rounded the side of the house, and she stopped, her eyes widening, her mouth gaping.

"Prince?" she whispered.

The gelding neighed loudly and tossed his black mane.

"Prince." Her breath caught and she looked at Sharif.

"He is yours," Sharif said quietly, holding her gaze. "He belongs to you. Just as I do."

Livy's knees threatened to buckle. "And I to you," she said, her heart brimming with emotion.

Because finally, she truly did belong.

Epilogue

Even if she'd had the power to do so, Rose couldn't have chosen a more glorious day for a wedding celebration in Balahar. The sky stretched across the country like an artist's blue canvas with brush strokes of salmon and pink marking the horizon. The day had been filled with wine and food and merriment, and so much love it made Rose's heart swell with pride and gratitude.

The people of Balahar and Sorajhee were excited over their recent unification and the protection it offered them from their enemies, and were even more jubilant to have Sharif as their new ruler. As far as their new queen, well, she just about had everyone eating out of her hand.

Rose smiled at Livy, leaning over the palace balcony to accept a bouquet of white roses from a grinning, toothless child. She made a stunning bride, her face glowing with happiness and excitement. Even though she and Sharif had already been married at the Desert Rose, the celebration today was for their subjects who stretched as far as the eye could see.

Of course that didn't stop the entire Coleman and El Jeved clans from following the newlywed couple across three continents to join in the second celebration. Rose's heart swelled at the sight of her family all standing behind Sharif and Livy.

Randy and Vi held hands and whispered like teenagers. Alex and Hannah stood off to the left, his arm around her while she stroked her swollen belly. Cade and Serena and Jessica all had their heads together. They were no doubt up to something. Rose hated to even guess after the beer dunking Sharif and Livy received at the Desert Rose ceremony. Only Mac and Abbie seemed subdued. Rose suspected it was because they'd decided to leave baby Sarah behind.

Sarah Rose Coleman–El Jeved—her very first grandchild. Rose sighed in blissful contentment.

Zak put his arm around her and kissed her temple. "That is a happy sigh, I trust."

"The happiest." She leaned against him and gazed out at her family, at the hordes of admiring subjects crowding the hillside leading to the palace, and the rainbow of flowers they had strewn around the palace walls as was custom. "She's such a beautiful bride, isn't she?"

"Yes, but not as beautiful as you will be next week."

"Oh, Zak." She flattened a palm on his chest and leaned her head on his shoulder. Could life possibly be any better? "Thank you for being patient and waiting. As anxious as I am to become your wife, this moment had to be for Sharif and Livy."

"I understand," he said, as they both turned toward the couple, Sharif staring with undisguised pride at his wife. "He is a man now. There were times I thought I would not live to see the day."

Rose laughed softly. "Did you know he went with Livy to visit the orphanage yesterday?"

Zak nodded. "He has made arrangements for the children to tour the palace and have lunch with them. I believe it was Olivia who suggested the pony rides after."

"The people love her."

"She has been good for them and Sharif."

Rose nodded, and then leaned forward to hear what Livy was saying to the child who'd given her the roses. Everyone within hearing distance had the strangest looks on their faces.

When Livy repeated the phrase, Rose bit her lip to keep from laughing. Neither Zak nor Sharif bothered to restrain themselves. Livy was still learning the language and didn't always get pronunciations right. Instead of saying thank you, she'd wished the girl bad teeth for life.

As word of what their new queen had said was passed from person to person down the hillside, the laughter came in waves. There was no mistaking the affection the people had for their new ruler and his bride.

Rose sighed again, and Zak tightened his hold.

"You know," he said, "I'm glad we decided to wait to wed. Olivia is a beautiful bride, but it wouldn't have been fair of you to show her up."

Rose smiled at his charming lie and snuggled closer. "Who said there are no fairy tale endings."

Coming in August from

and

Judy Christenberry

RANDALL PRIDE

HAR #885

She was the ultimate forbidden fruit. Surely now that
lovely Elizabeth was engaged to another man, it was
finally safe for Toby Randall to return home. But once
he arrived, the rodeo star realized that his love for
Elizabeth had only grown stronger and he'd let
no man stand between them.

**Don't miss this heartwarming addition
to the series**

Available wherever Harlequin books are sold.

Makes any time special ®

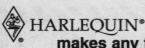

Harlequin truly does
make any time special. . . .
This year we are celebrating
weddings in style!

To help us celebrate, we want you to tell us how wearing the Harlequin wedding gown will make your wedding day special. As the grand prize, Harlequin will offer one lucky bride the chance to **"Walk Down the Aisle" in the Harlequin wedding gown!**

There's more...

For her honeymoon, she and her groom will spend five nights at the **Hyatt Regency Maui.** As part of this five-night honeymoon at the hotel renowned for its romantic attractions, the couple will enjoy a candlelit dinner for two in Swan Court, a sunset sail on the hotel's catamaran, and duet spa treatments.

To enter, please write, in, 250 words or less, how wearing the Harlequin wedding gown will make your wedding day special. The entry will be judged based on its emotionally compelling nature, its originality and creativity, and its sincerity. This contest is open to Canadian and U.S. residents only and to those who are 18 years of age and older. There is no purchase necessary to enter. Void where prohibited. See further contest rules attached. Please send your entry to:

Walk Down the Aisle Contest

In Canada	In U.S.A.
P.O. Box 637	P.O. Box 9076
Fort Erie, Ontario	3010 Walden Ave.
L2A 5X3	Buffalo, NY 14269-9076

You can also enter by visiting www.eHarlequin.com
Win the Harlequin wedding gown and the vacation of a lifetime!
The deadline for entries is October 1, 2001.

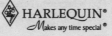